EMILY McKAY

Surrogate and Wife

Published by Silhouette Books
America's Publisher of Contemporary Romance

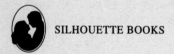 SILHOUETTE BOOKS

ISBN 0-373-76710-2

SURROGATE AND WIFE

Visit Silhouette Books at www.eHarlequin.com

Printed in U.S.A.

EMILY McKAY

has been reading romance novels since she was eleven years old. Her first Harlequin Romance novel came free in a box of Hefty garbage bags. She has been reading and loving romance novels ever since. She lives in Texas with her husband, her newborn daughter and too many pets. Her books have finaled in RWA's Golden Heart, the Write Touch Readers' Award and the Gayle Wilson Award of Excellence. Her debut novel, *Baby, Be Mine* was a RITA® Award finalist for Best First Book and Best Short Contemporary. To learn more, visit her Web site at www.EmilyMcKay.com.

To my wonderful sister, Robin, who dealt so bravely with her own fertility issues and who counseled me so wisely when I encountered problems of my own. Robin, I'm glad I didn't need to be a surrogate for you, but I would have done it in a second!

One

"We're pregnant."

Kate Bennet did her best not to roll her eyes at the absurdity of her sister's remark. "Yeah. I know."

As a surrogate mother for her sister, Beth, and her brother-in-law, Stewart, Kate knew all too well that "they" were pregnant. Her hand drifted to her belly where the baby was just beginning to show. Her stomach seemed to flip over, making her curse the first trimester nausea that had yet to fade. She picked up the mug of hot peppermint tea Beth had made for her.

Beth reached across the kitchen table and put her hand on Kate's wrist. Kate paused, mug halfway to her mouth. "What?"

"We're pregnant. Stew and I."

Kate lowered the mug, struggling to make sense of the words. "You and Stew?"

"Yes."

"Pregnant?"

Beth nodded, her smile so beatifically maternal her face all but glowed. Her eyes sparkled with happiness.

Kate's stomach did another flip, the nausea building now. She pressed her palm to her belly. "With another baby? In addition to the baby I'm carrying for you?"

"Yes."

Kate bolted from the chair and dashed to the hallway bathroom. She barely made it to the toilet bowl before emptying the remnants of her breakfast.

She knelt there for a long time on the bathroom floor, leaning against the cabinet, eyes pressed closed, until her stomach stilled and tile bruised her knees. Only the sound of Beth knocking on the door roused her from her stupor.

"Kate? Are you okay?"

Was she okay? Well, she felt as if her world had just been turned inside out—along with her stomach. Other than that, she was just ducky.

She hoisted herself to her feet to wash her hands and rinse out her mouth before opening the bathroom door. Resting her shoulder against the doorjamb, she stared at her sister. "How is this possible?"

Beth grasped her elbow and guided her away from the door and down the hallway. "Come back to the kitchen. I'll make you a fresh cup of tea."

Kate let herself be pushed gently into the Windsor chair and watched as Beth bustled around the simple, homey kitchen.

"We were as surprised as you," Beth said.

"But you and Stewart can't have children. It's impossible. Isn't it?"

"Highly improbable. But not impossible."

In fact, their chances were viewed as so slim, the doctor had recommended not using Stew's sperm to inseminate Kate. Instead, Stew had asked his best friend, Jake, to be a sperm donor.

Still reeling, Kate said, "I thought you said there was only a 0.2% chance of you getting pregnant on your own."

"We were just very lucky." Beth set a mug of steaming water in front of Kate and held out a bowl of teabags. "Peppermint or chamomile?"

"How can you be so calm?" Kate felt hysteria rising up inside her as the full implication of Beth's pregnancy began to sink in. Kate snatched one of the offered packages, ripped it open and dunked the teabag rapidly in and out of the water.

"I guess, because I've had more time to get used to the idea."

Kate's hand instantly stilled and her eyes sought Beth's face. "How long have you known?"

"A week. I suspected for longer, but I didn't dare hope. My periods have always been so irregular—and after so many years of trying—well, I'd trained myself not to hope, even when I missed a period. Or four."

"Four? How far along are you?"

"Eighteen weeks."

"Eighteen weeks? That's a full month further along than I am. A full month." The very thought made her mind whirl and she sank back against the chair. "So all those sympathetic pregnancy symptoms you've been going through that I thought were so charming weren't sympathetic ones at all. They were real."

Beth smiled wryly. "I hadn't thought of that." She reached for Kate's hand. "Look, I know this makes everything very complicated, but ultimately Stew and I just really want to be parents."

Kate sat forward. "You still want this baby, right?"

Beth gave her another beatific smile. "Well, Stew

and I talked about it and agreed that decision should be up to you and Jake."

"Up to me and Jake? What's that supposed to mean?"

"Technically, it's your baby and—"

"No. There's no technically about it." Okay, *technically* she was both egg donor and genetic carrier, so the baby was biologically hers, but still… "This baby is yours. Yours and Stew's. That was the agreement."

The tension inside Kate threatened to boil over. She leaped to her feet and began pacing, glancing incredulously at her sister. Under the circumstances, Beth didn't seem nearly as distressed as she should be.

Beth stood following Kate's movement with her gaze. "Yes, of course that was the agreement. But things have changed."

"You can't refuse to take this baby. I won't allow it." Kate spun around and pinned Beth with her most judicial stare. At least, she tried to pin Beth with a stare, but a wave of dizziness left her groping for a handhold on the nearby countertop, which ruined the effect.

Beth rushed immediately to her side. "Come and sit down. You shouldn't be pacing like that. It can't be good for the baby."

"You know what's not good for the baby?" she quipped irritably. "This whole conversation." Still, she sank gratefully into the chair.

"Naturally, Stew and I will still take the baby. If you decide you don't want it. But we want you to at least think about keeping it. The baby is biologically yours. And whether you're willing to admit it or not, you feel a connection to it already."

For a second, Kate didn't know what to say. Didn't Beth get it? Didn't she understand that the only way

Kate had been able to do this was by doing everything she could not to feel a connection to the baby?

"I don't—"

"I know you do," Beth said, cutting her off, "So there's no use arguing with me about it. The point is, we have two healthy babies here. Stew and I would love to have them both, but we knew all along we were asking a lot of you and Jake. So if either of you—"

"Jake? What's he have to do with this?"

Beth shot her an exasperated look. "That baby you're carrying is his, too. If either of you decides you want to keep the baby, Stew and I are willing to step aside."

Suddenly struck by the absurdity of the situation, Kate dropped her face into her hands and choked back laughter. "If either of us wants to keep the baby? You realize how completely absurd that is, don't you?"

But Beth, who merely looked at her with a slight frown, apparently did not.

"Let's face it," Kate explained. "I have all the maternal instincts of a paper clip. The only idea sillier than me wanting to keep the baby is Jake Morgan wanting to keep it. He's hardly 'daddy' material."

"Jake's not so bad," Beth protested.

"Hey, he may be a great guy, for all I know. But we're talking about a man who runs into burning buildings when everyone else runs out."

"Actually—" Beth lifted her chin stubbornly "—now that he's moved up to arson investigation, he doesn't run into burning buildings anymore. Just smoldering ones."

"Right. Smoldering ones. Big difference."

Beth flashed an impish grin. "Well, at least his kid won't play with matches."

Kate pointed a finger at her sister. "You can laugh now, but these are the genes your child is going to have."

Beth just chuckled. "I'm not worried about Jake's genes. He's smart, handsome, charming, and—"

"Exactly. He's one of those annoying people who thinks he should get whatever he wants just because he *is* handsome and charming." Hoping she hadn't revealed just how appealing she found Jake—or how much that annoyed her, she said quickly, "What does my opinion of Jake have to do with anything?

"It's not like you to be so judgmental."

Beth was right, of course. So Kate smiled wryly and said, "I'm a judge. We're supposed to be judgmental. Besides, I know I'm right about this. With all the broken homes and bad parents I see in my courtroom, it's my job to cull the good from the bad. I promise you, neither Jake nor I will want this baby."

"Just think about it. You might change your mind."

"Yes. And I might turn into a pig, sprout wings and fly. It's not impossible, just highly improbable."

Despite her determination to put it out of her mind, Kate was still thinking about her conversation with Beth the next evening as she tried to finish up paperwork at the office. It was after six on a Monday; nearly everyone else in the courthouse annex had gone home. But she'd long since given up any hope that the relative quiet would help her concentrate.

How could she not think about Beth's offer to let her keep the baby? Kate rested her hand upon her belly where her baby was growing inside.

Her baby.

Her breath caught in her throat as she felt emotion tighten her chest. For once she didn't try to squash it or shove it aside. What would happen if she did allow herself to keep the baby?

Her heart filled with anticipation. As if keeping the baby was what she'd been subconsciously hoping to do, even though every logical bone in her body had told her doing so would be selfish and irresponsible.

She already loved this baby. Even though it was too early to tell the baby's sex, Kate's gut told her the baby was a girl. Kate's gut had been pretty vocal lately. Every instinct she had demanded her baby girl would want for nothing. So Kate had spent the past three months following to the letter the advice not only of her doctor but also every pregnancy book she could get her hands on. By golly, this was going to be the happiest, healthiest baby ever born. And if she had anything to say about it, this baby would have the best of everything.

That included the best parents. Kate knew, beyond a shadow of a doubt, that Beth would be a much better mother than she would be.

She saw the evidence all the time in her family-law courtroom. Some women—like Beth—were born to be mothers. Others just weren't. In her professional opinion, Kate knew she fell into the latter group.

Suddenly angry with herself for dwelling on the issue for so long, she shoved the files she'd been reviewing into her briefcase and headed for the door. The brisk walk to her car made her feel no less grumpy. When she reached the parking lot to find *him* leaning against her Volvo, her mood plummeted even further.

She'd never quite been able to pin down what it was, but something about Jake Morgan just rubbed her the wrong way. It wasn't only his confident charm—a trait she'd learned long ago to neither like nor trust in men. Maybe it was that slow, sensual gaze of his that seemed to undress a woman and make love to her all at once. Or maybe it was just the pure testosterone that emanated from him in waves. He was just too much. Too masculine. Too charming. And entirely too smug.

Not to mention too in her way.

"What are you doing here?" she asked as she approached her car.

His long legs were crossed at the ankles. The faded denim of his jeans stretched taut across his thighs. His only defense against the unusually cold May evening was a long-sleeve flannel shirt worn unbuttoned over his T-shirt. With the sleeves rolled up, no less.

Typical. Probably thought he was too manly to need a coat. Or maybe he knew how good he looked and didn't want to ruin the effect.

She pulled her keys from her coat pocket and used the remote to pop the locks. With a shrug of his muscular shoulders, he pushed himself away from her car.

"I came to see you."

"I assumed as much." She opened the rear door and slid her briefcase onto the seat. She made no move to climb into the car herself. He was standing too close to the driver's door for her to comfortably edge past him. "You always lurk in parking lots by women's cars? That could be construed as stalking."

A slow smile spread across his face. "And here you always pretend not to have a sense of humor."

Even though she had been joking, his insinuation annoyed her. So she said, "I don't joke about that kind of thing."

"No, of course not." He faked a serious frown, but his twitching lips gave him away. "By the time I got here, the building was closed for the night."

"The guards usually leave at 5:30."

He nodded. "I figured as much. But this was my only free evening this week and I think we need to talk."

"Why?"

This time he chuckled. "Don't look so suspicious. I just want to talk about the situation with Beth and Stew."

"So talk."

"You really want to discuss this in the parking lot? We're just a block away from the restaurants on the square. Besides, it's too cold."

The thought of sharing a meal with Jake sent a shiver of apprehension through her. Georgetown, once a sleepy college town, had grown as the sprawl from Austin crept up IH 35. Like many small Texas towns overtaken by suburbia, Georgetown struggled to maintain its own identity. The historic town square, situated around the Williamson County Courthouse, with its collection of locally owned stores and restaurants was one of the ways Georgetown distinguished itself from larger, more liberal Austin.

While food sounded good to Kate, the romantic atmosphere of one of the local restaurants did not. Dinner was entirely too intimate. Too datelike. She sniffed dismissively. "Then you should have worn a coat."

"I meant for you. You're shivering already."

He was right, of course. Ever since the pregnancy, she'd been unusually cold. Which, for some reason, she didn't want to explain to him. Talking about pregnancy symptoms seemed even more intimate than dinner.

Suddenly she was aware how intimate their relationship already was. The bond they shared was so much deeper than just the sexual bond that usually accompanied intimacy. They'd created a life together.

A part of Jake was in her.

The thought unnerved her, so she fisted her hands on her lapels and pulled her jacket more closely around her body. She didn't want to eat dinner with him. Didn't want to do anything with him. Yet there probably were things they should talk about.

"Okay, then. Dinner it is."

Fifteen minutes later she found herself opposite him in a booth at one of the restaurants on the square, a mug of hot tea in front of her, a bowl of tortilla soup and a plate of cheese enchiladas on the way.

As she sipped her tea, she studied him over the rim of her mug. He sat in the middle of the bench with one arm stretched across the back, making his shoulders appear even wider so that he seemed to take up the entire booth.

Jake was so different from all the other men she knew. Men with manicured hands and suit jackets custom-made to make their shoulders appear wider than they were. Her gaze drifted down to Jake's hand where it rested, palm down on the Formica beside his beer. His hands were big, muscular even, with long tapered fingers that ended in clean but unmanicured nails. They were unquestionably masculine. Tough, almost.

Had she ever noticed a man's nails before? She didn't think so. There was something oddly personal about looking at Jake's hands. Warmth swirled through her body, pooling somewhere deep inside of her. Where she carried his baby.

She jerked her gaze back to his, cursing the blush she could feel on her cheeks. His eyes were practically gleaming with amusement. As if he could read her thoughts and knew just how unsettled he made her feel.

A scowl settled on her face and she sat up straighter. "Don't—"

"Let me stop you right there," he interrupted. "We both know you don't like me."

"I don't know you well enough to like you or not," she protested.

"Okay, don't *approve* of me."

Well, she couldn't really argue with that. They'd only met on a handful of occasions and she'd never been able to relax around him. She saw right through his laidback charm to the testosterone-fueled masculinity beneath. It was less that she didn't approve of him and more that she simply didn't know what to do with him. Which made her very nervous. She also couldn't deny how drawn to him she felt. Why now? Why Jake of all people?

Maybe this sudden attraction she felt was just some weird pregnancy thing. Maybe her body somehow knew he was the father of the child she carried. If that was the case, all the more reason to maintain her distance.

So she stiffened her spine as well as her resolve, and said, "No, I don't."

"Regardless of that, we're in this together now."

"I disagree. If anyone is in this together, it's Beth, Stewart and me. Your part in this is, thankfully, over."

"That might have been true before, but now—"

"Nothing is different now."

"You can't really be that naive."

She bristled at his words, even though there was nothing objectionable in his tone. She leaned forward over the table. "Trust me. I am anything but naive. I understand exactly—"

"Okay, not naive then." He held up his hands in a gesture of innocence. "But you've got to admit, things are going to be a lot different than any of you planned."

"Yes, they'll be different, but I'll manage."

He continued as if he hadn't heard her concession. "You were planning on Beth and Stew helping you out. Taking care of you. Things are going to be different now. They've got their own pregnancy to contend with."

"You think I can't take care of myself? Trust me, I've

been doing it for years. Far longer than most women my age, actually."

"That's not what I meant."

"Then what did you mean?"

"From what Beth has said, you haven't had an easy first trimester, but it's only going to get worse. The second trimester won't be too bad, but by the time you hit the third trimester, you'll—"

"What makes you such an expert? Have you taken some sort of course in prenatal care?"

He grimaced. "No, but five of my buddies have had babies in the past eighteen months. I've heard my share of complaints about late-night cravings and women who can't tie their own shoelaces."

"Well, unless you're planning on moving in with me, I don't see how you could help with either one of those situations." She chuckled, but the sound died in her throat when she realized he wasn't laughing with her. "Oh my God. You can't be serious." She gaped at him in disbelief, waiting for him to crack a smile and laugh at her expense. He didn't even blink. "You *are* serious. You think we should move in together."

Two

Kate jerked away from him and shrank back into the booth. "Are you insane?"

Okay, that could have gone a little more smoothly.

"Just hear me out—"

"I mean, I knew you were crazy in that, anyone-willing-to-run-into-a-burning-building kind of way, but *this?*"

Okay, a lot more smoothly.

"Or are you joking? Because this just isn't funny."

"I'm not joking. And if you'll just give me a chance to explain—"

But before he could, the waitress approached with their food.

Kate fumed in silence while their plates were distributed, glaring at him from across the table as if wishing she could charge him with contempt of court.

"Okay, talk," she ordered as soon as the waitress was out of earshot. "But make it good, because I'm having a hard time believing that you've been nursing a secret desire to cater to the whims of a second-trimester pregnant woman."

She continued her diatribe for a solid four more minutes. He didn't bother interrupting—she wouldn't have let him, anyway. Instead, he took the opportunity to study her.

With her ivory complexion and thick black hair pulled back from her face, he'd have to be dead not to notice how beautiful she was. She wasn't anything like the women he normally dated, but she piqued his interest. Smart, sexy and fiercely independent. Challenging enough to keep things interesting without ever being clingy or emotionally demanding.

Not that he'd dream of pursuing her now. That would only screw up an already complicated situation. To make matters worse, he couldn't help admiring how she resisted his help. Even though it made things more difficult for him.

"I wouldn't have to actually move in," he pointed out once she seemed to lose steam. "But I could still help out." Changing tactics, he said, "Beth and Stew are worried about you."

She rolled her eyes. "Beth and Stew always worry about me. Trust me, if it wasn't this, it'd be something else. The part of town I live in or the hours I work. Beth is a worrier."

"Well, this time she feels responsible." He leaned forward, bracing his elbows on either side of his plate. "Whether you like it or not, your life is changing. I can help you."

"What exactly is it you think I need help with?"

"Whatever." He shrugged. "Laundry, grocery shopping, cooking. The point is, you don't have to be so stubborn. You don't have to do everything on your own."

Her eyes flashed as she leaned forward and spoke with barely concealed annoyance. "I'm not being stubborn. I *can* take care of myself. I am not your problem. I—"

He recognized the slipup as soon as the words were out of her mouth. The way she broke off, then pulled away from the table to toy with her napkin as if flustered, only confirmed that she hadn't meant to give so much away.

Maybe he should have just let it go, but he couldn't resist digging a little. I never said *you* were."

She wiped her fingers on her napkin and tossed it to the side of her plate. "Fine. The *baby* is not your problem. None of this has anything to do with you."

"Ah, come on. Even *you* have to admit it has at least a little to do with me."

She waved her hand dismissively. "Yes, yes, your part was very important. I certainly didn't mean to belittle your contribution of spending thirty minutes in a locked room with a plastic cup, but I daresay you've done enough. This end of the deal—" she gestured to her belly "—is all my responsibility."

Suddenly he didn't feel like teasing her anymore. "You don't have to do it all on your own."

She cleared her throat. He could practically see her struggling for a flip response, but in the end, her answer came out sounding as serious as his had. "Yes, I do."

"But—"

"Look, even if your intentions are good, we're talking about the next six months of your life. You're bound to get bored of playing house."

"I'm not—"

"I didn't mean that as an insult," she reassured him. "We're talking about half a year of giving up your spare time to coddle a pregnant woman. You'd have to be a saint to do that. And, let's face it, you're no saint."

"You have no idea," he said, unable to shake from his consciousness all the sinful things he'd like to do to her.

He knew this discussion was affecting her as much as it did him, because her voice sounded brusque when she replied, "Which only proves my point. Do you really think you're going to want to spend your time off doing *my* laundry when you could be out on a date? Right now, all this pregnancy stuff may seem fascinating, but, trust me, the novelty will wear off."

"And you think I won't stick around after the novelty wears off."

"I'm not about to start depending on you now, only to find out you won't."

He leaned back in his seat and stretched his arm across the back of the booth. "You don't have a very high opinion of me, do you?"

"Don't take it personally. There aren't a lot of people I do have a high opinion of."

"That's a pretty cynical attitude."

"Not cynical. Realistic. Every day at work, I see people at their absolute worst. I know what men—and women—are capable of. How they can hurt and betray the people they claim to love the most. If there's one thing I've learned after four years on the bench, it's that the only person you can really trust is yourself."

"What about Beth and Stew?"

"Of course I trust them. But I certainly don't expect them to take care of me. Especially not now that they've got their own baby on the way. I'll be fine on my own. Just like I've always been."

And with that she grabbed her purse, dropped a twenty on the table and scooted out of the booth. She left the restaurant without even a backward glance.

He stared at the money for a minute before the irony

sank in. This was the biggest commitment he'd ever tried to make to a woman and she hadn't even let him buy her dinner.

After he dropped his own twenty on the table, he pulled his cell phone from his pocket and dialed Stew.

"You were right," he said as soon as Stew answered.

"I told you she wouldn't go for it."

"She sounded insulted."

Stew chuckled. "Of course she was insulted. Basically, you told a grown woman you thought she couldn't take care of herself. Not just any grown woman, either. This is Kate we're talking about here. She's been on her own a long time and she's always prided herself on her competence. Which you just questioned."

"Not exactly." At least, he didn't think he had. "I think she doesn't like me."

"No, she probably doesn't. You haven't made a very good impression on her."

Great. Of all the women he'd known in his life, and gotten along with just fine, the one who didn't like him at all was the one carrying his baby.

He'd been eight years younger and stupider when they first met. Too young to know that some women found charm suspicious. It hadn't helped that she'd been so much fun to tease. She'd never gotten past that first impression of him and he'd never made the effort to convince her he wasn't a total jerk.

"What're you going to do now?" Stew asked.

"Not much I can do. The ball's in her court. If she can't see the logic of my offer, there's nothing I can do about it." Then he muttered, "Why couldn't she be more like Beth? Beth would have said yes."

Stew chuckled. "Because Beth is a one-of-a-kind woman."

So was Kate, Jake couldn't help thinking a few minutes later as he tucked the phone back into his pocket and made his way to his car.

Kate was unlike any woman he'd ever met. Tough, cynical and stubborn. Boy, she was stubborn.

He knew he was right—she would need help in the coming months—but he had no idea how to convince her of that. Still, he couldn't help admiring her for clinging so passionately to her independence. She was a complex and intriguing woman. Way too intriguing.

Under the circumstances, he should probably be thanking his lucky stars she'd refused his offer. He was off the hook. Not even Stewart could say he hadn't tried.

So why couldn't he shake the feeling that something really important had just slipped through his fingers?

He couldn't explain—not even to himself—why he wanted so desperately to be a part of this pregnancy. Surely his offer to help Kate was nothing more than that. Help. It certainly didn't have anything to do with this inexplicable pull she suddenly had over him.

Shaking his head, he shoved the thought aside. As he steered his car toward home, he knew he should be rejoicing in his freedom. And he didn't let himself wonder why he wasn't.

Her week—which had started out so badly—only got worse.

From the news about Beth's pregnancy, to the bizarre dinner with Jake, to this—being called on the carpet by Judge Hatcher first thing Thursday morning.

Two years ago Hatcher had been elected a district judge on a platform of conservative family values. Since associate district judges like Kate were merely appointed, Hatcher was essentially her boss. She wasn't happy about it, since they shared years of barely concealed animosity, dating all the way back to when they'd both worked in the Georgetown D.A.'s office. However, since he had the power to make her life very difficult, and since she knew this position was only a stepping-stone to further his political ambitions, she'd stayed out of his way. Until now.

As she made her way back to her chambers in the courthouse annex, she struggled to calm herself. She found Kevin Thompson, the other associate district judge, waiting for her, noisily poking through the papers on her desk.

"How'd it go?"

Still feeling bristly, she glared at him. "How did you know about my meeting with Hatcher?"

"Are you kidding? In this office, gossip spreads like wildfire."

She grimaced. As if she needed that reminder.

Kevin propped himself on the edge of her desk. "So, how did the meeting go? Did he just want to rake you over the coals a little?"

"It went about the same as all my meetings with him go. He was patronizing and rude. I kept my mouth shut."

"Good girl. I know he drives you crazy, but it's best to keep your head down and your nose clean. And look at it this way, in six months he'll be out of here."

She sank into her chair. "That's not reassuring. In six months the elections will be over. If he's out of here, that means he's been elected to the Texas Supreme Court."

Kevin shrugged. "True, but at least he'll be out of our hair. And let's face it, ever since he announced he was running, he's been a pain in the patootie."

Kate sighed. That was sure the truth.

Meeting Kevin's gaze, she said, "He wants me to step aside and let him handle the McCain case."

Kevin let out a low whistle. "Guess we should have seen that coming. Are you going to do it?"

"Step aside? No. Not if I can help it. That case has been on my docket for months now."

"A high profile divorce like that? To be honest, I'm surprised this is the first time it's come up."

Roger and Shelia McCain had worked for a local personal computer company during the boom. The millions they'd made thrust them into the local limelight. Everyone in town wanted to know the details of their divorce settlement. "Until recently, it's only made the local weekly," she reasoned. "But now that the story is being picked up by the *Austin American-Statesman* and the *Houston Chronicle*, he can't resist getting the press. Guess he figures it's good for the campaign."

"Good for the campaign? That kind of daily press would be worth a fortune. Maybe you should just let him handle it."

She shot Kevin an incredulous look. "And let that viper turn those poor people's divorce into a media circus about waning family values? Think about what that would do to them. Worse still to their kids. I'm not going to give him the case unless I don't have any other options."

"Oh, honey." Kevin shook his head slowly. "Just be careful."

"I won't be bullied by him," she insisted. "Sure, he can make my life difficult, but that won't further his political ambitions."

Kevin raised his eyebrows pointedly, as if she'd missed something obvious.

"What else can he do?" she asked with false cheer. "It's not like he can fire me." Her chuckle died in her throat when Kevin didn't join in. "You think he's going

to fire me? That's ridiculous. Even *he* wouldn't try to
have someone removed from the bench. Would he?"

"I think if you gave him a reason to he would. Especially if he could pin you with something morally questionable. Think about it, you'd be the first associate
district judge fired in over forty years. It'd be all over
the press, so it'd be a chance to remind everyone of the
hyperconservative values he stands for."

She studied her friend. "Are you worried about
your job?"

"Me?" He shrugged. "Not really. I'm very careful,
and you're the only one around here who knows." Kevin
didn't dare utter the word *gay* in these conservative
halls. "Besides, it's not me he hates. And if he gets rid
of you, he could swoop in, take over the McCain case
and maximize his media exposure."

As she listened to Kevin, she felt a sinking sensation
deep in her stomach. What if he was right? What if
Hatcher was just looking for a reason to fire her?

She'd been perfectly behaved, perfectly respectable
her entire life. Except…

Except now she was pregnant. With no plans of
marrying.

Back when she'd first agreed to be Beth and Stew's
surrogate, it had seemed a simple enough matter. Of
course, that was a full five months ago, before
Hatcher had announced his plans to run for the
Supreme Court. Yes, it had occurred to her that some
of her more conservative colleagues might raise their
eyebrows, but surely no one could fault her for being
a surrogate mother for her sister. But now that Beth
was pregnant herself, would people question Kate's
pregnancy?

Kevin must have read the distress on her face, but he

hastened to reassure her. "Don't worry, hon. You're way too smart to give him a reason."

Kevin's reassurances did little to pacify her fears. "What if I had done something wrong?"

"You?" Kevin raised his eyebrows. "Little Miss Perfect you? You haven't made a misstep in decades."

"Hypothetically, let's say I did do something…questionable in Hatcher's view. He's just one judge. Wouldn't he have to convince the other seven district judges in order to get me removed?"

"I'd say it all depends on whether they think your 'questionable' behavior impairs your abilities or position of authority. In this conservative political environment, it might not take much. Especially with Hatcher focusing his campaign on moral values. The last thing the other judges want is to appear morally lax. Good thing for you you're squeaky clean, right?"

She smiled lamely and hoped it didn't look too much like a grimace. "Right. Lucky me."

By the time Kevin left for court, Kate's head was reeling. All she could do was stare numbly at her desk, asking herself over and over again, Could he be right?

Unfortunately, the only answer she could come up with was *Yes*. Very soon she was going to appear to be an unmarried mother-to-be. That seemed like exactly the kind of morally questionable behavior Hatcher would use against her.

Three

Standing outside Jake's apartment, waiting for him to answer the door, Kate was practically shaking in her boots. Or she would have been if she'd been wearing boots. As it was, she was merely shaking in her sensible, size-nine black pumps.

"Can we talk?" she blurted out when the door finally opened.

Jake stared at her blankly for a long moment.

Long enough for her to be reminded how handsome he was. How purely masculine. Of course, it didn't help matters that he was bare-chested.

But the thing that really got to her, that actually made her heart stop beating for a second, was how the sheer size of him made her feel feminine. Delicate. Almost frail, even.

She was a solid five-nine, barefoot. No one made her feel delicate.

No one except Jake.

She didn't like the feeling one bit. And she couldn't help wishing that Beth and Stewart had picked some other man to be the donor. Someone who didn't make her feel so distinctly at a disadvantage. Preferably someone who didn't make her feel anything.

Someone who didn't look as if he'd just tumbled out of bed.

"Oh, God," she muttered, finally breaking the silence. "You're not alone." The naked chest, the disheveled hair, the sleepy stupor. She'd have put it all together sooner if she hadn't been so distracted by the…well, the naked chest and disheveled hair. Mortification spread through her and she spun on her heel to leave. "I'll come back another time. Or better yet, just forget I ever came here."

But before she could make it even a few steps, he grabbed her by the arm.

"Oh, no, you don't. You got me out of bed. You might as well say whatever it is you came here to say."

"I…"

He pulled her into the apartment, not roughly, but with enough force to remind her—again—how much stronger he was. Toeing the door shut, he wheeled her around to face him.

"I, um…" she began again, only to have all thoughts evaporate the instant she realized how close she was to his bare chest.

"What's wrong? You look…sick, or something."

Or something, indeed. "I'm a little faint," she lied, pulling her arm from his grasp. "I've been having dizzy spells lately." Which wasn't entirely untrue. He did make her head spin.

He reached for her arm again, carefully steering her to the nearby leather sofa. "You should sit. Can I get you something to drink? Water? No, wait, milk. Can I get you a glass of milk?"

Great. Here she was wrestling with this unexpected attraction to him, and he wanted to make sure she was properly hydrated. Just great.

"No, nothing. Look, I'm sorry I interrupted your…evening. I should have called first."

"You didn't interrupt anything. I was asleep." He smiled wryly as he grabbed a flannel shirt that had been left dangling over the back of a chair. He slipped into the shirt, buttoning enough for modesty, but not enough to block the occasional glimpse of his muscles. "Alone."

"Oh. I see." Except she wasn't sure she did. It was Friday night. And it was only nine-thirty.

He must have noticed her looking at her watch because he explained, "I have to be at the firehouse pretty early in the morning."

"Oh. Then I'm sorry I—"

"Why don't you stop apologizing and go back to the part where you said we need to talk."

He lowered himself into the club chair beside the sofa. Again he seemed entirely too close.

"I…um…" The words caught in her throat, trapped there by a giggle rising to the surface. This was absurd, but so was the question she couldn't see a way out of asking. So finally she just said, "Will you marry me?"

Jake froze, his expression blank for the second time this evening. Then shock registered, and his voice rose sharply as he asked, "What?"

"I need to get married." Then she added in a rush, "And you did offer to help out with the pregnancy. You said you'd do anything you could."

"I meant I'd help with your laundry. I didn't think you'd want to get married."

"You said you would help."

"Sure, but married? You want to get married?"

"It'd be a marriage in name only," she reassured him. "Just until after the baby is born. Maybe not even that long."

"Let me see if I've got this right. Four days ago you didn't even want me to do your grocery shopping, and now you want to get married?"

"Yes. Well, not exactly." She frowned, trying to sort through the logic of her proposal. "See, here's the thing. There's a slight chance that if I have this baby out of wedlock, I'll be fired."

She watched his expression carefully, looking for any hint of his emotions, but he remained stoic. After several seconds he asked, "How slight?"

"Slight-ish."

"Can you give it to me in a percentage?"

"Maybe forty…" She paused, then added honestly. "Ninety percent."

For another several seconds, he stared at her, then he sprang to his feet and marched to the kitchen. She heard him open and close the refrigerator door. A minute later he reappeared with a bottle of beer, half of which was already gone, as if he'd had to take several fortifying gulps before facing her again.

He rested his shoulder against the doorway to the kitchen and leveled his gaze at her. "So there's a 'slight' ninety percent chance you'll get fired when you have this baby and you didn't think to mention it until now?"

"I didn't think it wasn't an issue before Beth and Stew got pregnant." As briefly as she could, she explained about Hatcher's bid for a seat on the Texas Supreme Court and his moral-values campaign. "So you see, being a surrogate mother for your sister who can't get pregnant could be considered noble. Claiming to be a surrogate for your sister who's already noticeably more pregnant than you is definitely suspicious."

He eyed her doubtfully. "You really think anyone will even notice that you and Beth are pregnant at the same time?"

"Yes, I do. Beth and Stew know a lot of people. Half the town shops in their health food store. Trust me, people are going to notice she's pregnant."

"So, you just have to explain the situation. Most people will believe you."

She sighed. "You're right, of course. Most people will. But Hatcher doesn't have to convince 'most people' in order to get me fired."

"Do you have some kind of morality clause or something in your contract?"

"I'm an associate district judge," she explained. "We're appointed by the district judges. We don't have contracts."

"This Judge Hatcher can just fire you on a whim? His decision doesn't have to be based on your performance? That's bull."

"I couldn't agree more." Even under the circumstances, she couldn't help being a little amused by his vehement reaction. "Of course, it's not his decision alone. There are eight district judges total. They'd have to vote on it. All Hatcher really has to do is call a press conference questioning my morality. A public outcry from a few concerned citizens would be enough. He only needs a simple majority to vote me out of office. That's just four other people."

"And you think he can convince them?"

"I think it's possible. He doesn't even have to convince them that what I've done is wrong. He just has to convince them that supporting me could risk their reputations. With reelections right around the corner, how many judges do you think will stand against him?"

Jake didn't answer, but the clenching of his jaw muscle said it all. The situation pissed him off almost as much as it did her.

"He'll have to convince the other district judges that I'm morally unfit to preside over a court of law, but—" she shrugged "—Williamson County is one of the most conservative counties in the state, maybe even the country. If there's anywhere being labeled an unwed mother could cost me my job, it's here."

He didn't argue with her, which only confirmed that she was right. The simple truth was that people held judges to a higher standard of behavior. And Kate, for one, expected no less.

"I still don't see how our getting married will help things. You think people will notice that you and Beth are pregnant at the same time, but not notice six months from now when we get divorced and they adopt your child? You don't think anyone will question your morality then?"

"That's just it," she countered. "By the time I have the baby in November, the elections will be over. Regardless of the outcome, Hatcher could no longer use me as a pawn in his or anyone else's campaign." She sensed she'd almost swayed him, so she added, "It'd only be until November."

After a long moment of studying her, he shook his head ruefully. "Look, the situation sucks, but—"

She stood. "You said you would help."

"I know I did, but—"

She crossed the room until she was standing right in front of him. "You said you would do anything you could to help out."

"I know. And you said you didn't trust me to stick around."

"So prove me wrong." She met his gaze head-on. As disturbing as it was to stare into his eyes at this range, she didn't let herself blink.

"What makes you think I'll make an even halfway decent husband?"

"I don't need you to be a decent husband. I just need a ceremony and a ring."

He chuckled. "Lowered your standards a bit, have you?"

"Don't make this harder than it is."

If possible, his smile broadened. Apparently whatever panic he'd initially felt had dissipated. "Why shouldn't I? You certainly made my initial offer to help difficult."

Only Jake could find humor in *this* situation. "I was surprised," she said through gritted teeth. "That's all."

"'Are you insane?' I believe those were your words."

Hearing him parrot her words back to her, she felt ashamed by how badly she'd treated him. Yet he didn't seem hurt. Didn't even seem angry. If anything, he seemed amused.

"Don't you take anything seriously?" she asked, suddenly feeling peevish.

"Very little."

"Not even insults to your mental stability?"

He just shrugged. "I've heard a lot worse than anything you can come up with, Katie."

She spun on her heel, needing to put distance between them. "This is never going to work. You're not the crazy one. I am."

But before she could make a move, he was beside her, his hand on her shoulder, easing her back to her spot on the sofa. "Hey, calm down. I was just teasing."

"Well, stop. This isn't the time or the place. What we're talking about is very serious."

"If you say so."

"I do say so." She desperately wanted to jump to her feet and pace. But doing so would probably mean being touched by him again. Since she wasn't willing to risk that, she scooted to the far corner of the sofa, then crossed her legs to keep herself from tapping her foot. "If we're going to do this, we need to be as businesslike about this as possible. We need rules. Boundaries."

Shirts that buttoned all the way up, she thought, wisely keeping it to herself.

"Gee, you're just suckin' all the fun right out of this."

If his amused expression was an indication, she hadn't sucked any of the fun out of it for him.

"I'm serious."

"I know you are. That's what makes it so damn cute."

"Cute?" She wasn't cute. No one called her cute. She was a judge, for goodness' sake. Judges weren't cute. She was pretty sure that edict had been written into the Texas Constitution.

"Now, don't get all huffy on me," he said in his most placating tone.

"I am not getting huffy."

"Sure you are."

"No, I'm—" She sucked in a deep breath. "This is exactly why we need boundaries."

"This?" he asked archly.

"This." She waved her hand back and forth between them. "If any kind of arrangement between us is going to work, we can't have this kind of flirtatious banter."

He raised an eyebrow, studying her with obvious humor. "Flirtatious banter? So you think I'm flirting with you?"

Despite his teasing manner, there was a spark of intensity deep in his gaze that unsettled her even more than his flirting.

Boundaries, she reminded herself. Get back to setting boundaries.

"I think you'll flirt with any woman within earshot." He didn't seem insulted by the observation. Or perhaps he just didn't see it as an insult. "But I don't want you to flirt with me. It would lend too much intimacy to the marriage."

"'Too much intimacy to the marriage.' Now there's a phrase you don't hear very often."

"And while we're on the subject…" She felt her throat beginning to tighten, and paused just long enough to clear it. Discreetly, she hoped. "I'm sure you'll agree there should be absolutely no…intimacy between us."

His lips twitched as if he was barely containing his laughter. "No intimacy? You mean like no flirting? You already covered that."

"No, I mean no intimacy." She felt her cheeks begin to burn. Damn it, why should this discussion embarrass her? She was a grown woman, for goodness sake. "No physical intimacy."

She'd forced herself to say the words without hesitating or stuttering. But she couldn't force her mind not to stumble over the images automatically produced. The two of them together, lying naked in a tangle of sheets.

Her reaction surprised her. She didn't want Jake Morgan. She *couldn't* want him. Not in their present situation. Not ever.

The only thing that surprised her more than her reaction was the flash of corresponding heat she saw in his gaze.

In an instant it was gone. Replaced by a teasing twinkle in his eye and a cocksure grin on his lips.

"So you think I won't be able to resist you? You

think once we're living together, we'll both cave to temptation unless we set up all these rules beforehand?"

"Certainly not. It just seemed wise to— Wait a minute, what do you mean once we're living together?"

"Well, there's no point in us getting married if people aren't going to see us living together, right? I was thinking your place, 'cause I assume it's bigger, but if you want to bunk down here, be my guest. But I've got to warn you, in your condition, I don't really think you should be sleeping on the sofa, and there's only one bed. I may be willing to give up my social life for this, but I'm not willing to give up my bed."

Her mind reeled as he babbled on about the comforts of his bed. He wanted them to *live* together? How could she possibly maintain her equilibrium—her emotional distance—with him living under her roof?

"No. Absolutely not." She shook her head, hoping she sounded very judicial, hoping her tone brooked no argument. "Cohabitation has disaster written all over it."

Either he didn't pick up on her no-one-argues-with-the-judge attitude, or he just didn't care. Because he said, just as firmly, "No, if we're going to do this, we're going to do it right. If we're legally married, but don't live together, that's way too suspicious. Hatcher—or someone else—will figure out something's wrong."

"You're right, of course." She sighed with resignation. "So what now?"

"We'll need to have a real ceremony," he said. It doesn't have to be in a church if you don't want it to, but we'll both have to invite some friends. Preferably friends from work, so that plenty of people will know. We'll need a story for how we met and why we're getting married so quickly. We can mention the baby if you want, but we don't want it to look like that's the only reason we're getting married."

"Not the only reason? You can't expect people to believe we're actually in love."

"That's exactly what I expect them to believe. For this to work, we need to *make* people believe it."

Four

In less than a week she'd be married.

They'd tentatively scheduled the wedding for Friday at the courthouse. She'd make the appointment Monday when she went in to work. Sure, being married by a J.P. lacked romance, but in this case that wasn't a bad thing. Besides, it had the added benefit of guaranteeing that everyone she worked with would know about the wedding within hours, Hatcher and the other district judges included.

But no matter how many times she told herself this was the only solution, it did nothing to diminish the sinking feeling in her belly. Or her racing thoughts. She was getting married. To Jake Morgan of all people!

Sunday night, as she lay in bed, trying to sleep, she couldn't keep that one terrifying thought from pounding through her head.

She'd gone to bed early, exhausted from spending the

day emptying out her spare room for Jake. Despite her protests, he'd insisted on giving up his apartment entirely, since it would look suspicious to keep it. So all of his furniture would be incorporated into her house or kept in the storage shed out back. After all her work she'd been sure her fatigue would take over and allow her to sleep. Yet here she lay, eyes wide open, heart beating too fast, thoughts racing too quickly for sleep to settle over her.

She felt so jittery, she actually jumped when the phone rang. Alarm shot through her as she snatched the phone from its cradle.

"Stew?"

"No, it's Jake." His voice sounded low and lazy through the phone lines. "Were you expecting Stew to call?"

Soothed by the tone of his voice, she sank back against her pillow. "No. But usually no one calls this late, so…never mind. It's silly."

"So you assumed something was wrong with Beth?"

"Yes." You only needed one alarming late-night phone call to fear them for life, and she'd had several. Mostly when she was young and she and Beth still lived with their mother. She didn't like that he found her so transparent, so she quickly changed the subject. "Did you need something, Jake?"

"I'm sorry I called. I wouldn't have done it if I'd known it would upset you."

"I'm not upset," she lied.

"In my defense, it's not that late."

She glanced at her bedside clock. Only 9:23. Dang it, he was right. Most people were still up watching the Sunday night movie.

"But I guess," he continued without waiting for her response, "that pregnant women tire easily and go to bed early. These are the kinds of things I'll have to get used to."

Now that was a disconcerting thought. "Why did you call, Jake?"

"I was thinking about our story."

In the background she could hear the faint murmur of a TV. "Our story?" she asked.

The sounds faded, as if he'd just turned down the volume with the remote. "The story of how we met, remember? We need to get our story straight, because when people find out we're getting married, they're bound to ask."

She could picture him so clearly in her mind. Lounging on that leather sofa, his legs stretched out onto the battered wood coffee table, phone in one hand, remote in the other, football game on ESPN.

Shaking her head to rid herself of the image, she said, "That's easy. We met at Beth and Stew's wedding."

"We met at their wedding eight years ago and now— outta nowhere—we're getting married? Naw, that doesn't make sense." He chuckled. "I bet you're a terrible liar."

Lying in the dark, she felt distinctly disadvantaged. So she flipped on the light beside her bed, stacked a couple of spare pillows behind her and sat up. "I'm a judge. We're not supposed to be good liars."

"Is that part of the job description?" he teased.

"No, but it should be," she said wryly. And then felt annoyed with herself for letting him lure her off the subject. "About this story, we should keep it as simple as possible. And close to the truth, if we can. If you think we really need one."

"Come on, everybody's got a story. And when a couple gets married, everyone wants to hear it."

"I disagree. Not everyone has an interesting story, and surely few people care enough to ask about it."

"How did Beth and Stew meet?" he asked.

"I don't know." She rubbed her temple as she thought about it. "I guess it was their freshman year at UT. She was working at that little sandwich shop across from campus." She couldn't keep from smiling as a few of the details came back to her. "Even though he was vegetarian, he'd always order a Philly cheesesteak, because they took so long to make and that gave him more time to talk to— Wait a second. Surely you've heard this all before."

Jake chuckled. "Of course I have, but you just proved my point. Everybody has a story."

"Maybe," she reluctantly admitted.

"Definitely. Tell me something. How did your parents meet?"

Kate chewed lightly on her lip, unsure what to say. Her parents had met in a bar during one of her mother's frequent bouts of drunkenness. Nine months later, when Kate was born, her mom couldn't remember her lover's name. Couldn't narrow the field of possible fathers down to just one guy, for that matter. The most Kate had ever been able to get out of her mom was, "He was probably either the cop from Austin or the salesman from Dallas. Or the trucker from Ohio."

Whichever guy it was, it didn't make for the kind of story she wanted to share. So she lied.

"They were high school sweethearts. Their first date was the homecoming dance. They married young." It wasn't entirely a lie. More an amalgamation of stories from her adopted parents and her various foster parents.

Since it would never hold up under questioning, she asked, "What about your parents? How did they meet?"

He didn't answer right away, and she thought she heard a refrigerator door open and then close on his end of the line. A second later she heard him take a drink.

Probably of beer. Instantly she pictured him standing with his shoulder propped against the kitchen doorway, the way he'd stood the other night.

Why did he feel the need to get a beer before answering such a simple question? Was it possible she wasn't the only one prevaricating about her past?

"Jake?" she prodded. Then felt guilty for being so nosy. And for jumping to conclusions. "Never mind. You don't have to tell me."

"Actually, he rescued her from a burning building. Saved her life."

"Really?" Now that she hadn't seen coming.

"Yeah, really. It was…"

When he didn't speak for several seconds, she offered, "Very romantic, I imagine."

She could picture it. The terror of being trapped in a burning building. The certainty that death was near. And then, out of the smoke, appears a handsome, broad-shouldered firefighter come to carry the damsel in distress to safety. It was the stuff of fantasies.

"Romantic? Sure. But it's a really bad way to start a relationship. When my dad was injured in the line of duty and had to take early retirement, I think my mom was more upset than he was. I don't think she ever forgave him for being just a man."

Something in his voice tugged at a part of her deep inside. He sounded so serious. So pensive.

This vulnerability disconcerted her. She didn't know how to talk to him when he was like this. Didn't know how to keep up her barriers against him. So she said nothing.

There was another long pause from his end of the phone. More sounds of him swallowing.

The image of him drinking from a beer bottle crept into her head again. She could practically see him. The way he tipped his head back. The way his Adam's apple slid up and down the column of his neck as he swallowed. The beads of condensation that formed on the bottle, moistening his fingers.

She wasn't a fanciful person. In fact, she'd been accused on more than one occasion of having no imagination at all. So why couldn't she turn off the images of Jake in her mind?

Was it merely the unnatural intimacy that came from talking to him on the phone while lying in bed?

That must be it.

"Look, I should go." She glanced at the clock. "Now it really is late. At least for a pregnant woman."

"Yeah, I suppose so—wait, we don't have a story yet."

"Can't it wait till tomorrow? We could talk after work."

"By then it'll be too late. You're making our appointment with the justice of the peace tomorrow, right?"

"Yes. I was going to do it over lunch."

"When you do, the women you work with will want details."

"The women I work with? What's that supposed to mean?"

"Oh, come on, don't pretend to be offended." That teasing warmth was back in his voice. "Women are the worst about this kind of thing."

She opened her mouth to disagree, then snapped it closed. He was right, of course. There would be at least a dozen women at the courthouse pumping her for information the second she scheduled an appointment with the J.P. Her court clerk, Meg. All the female court reporters. Not to mention the other judges. And Kevin would be just as bad as any of the women.

Did she dare share the truth with even him? If she did, there would be the inevitable questions about why she hadn't told him about the pregnancy in the first place. What a mess.

"You've gotten pretty quiet over there. You fall asleep?"

I wish.

"Okay, so we need a story by tomorrow. Surely you have some idea already or you wouldn't have brought it up."

"What about Beth and Stew's New Year's Eve party?"

"What about it?"

"We could say we 'fell in love' that night. We were both there, right?"

"Yes." She went every year, even though she normally didn't enjoy large parties. But on New Year's Eve it just seemed wrong to stay home watching repeats of *Law & Order.* "But so were about fifty other people. All of whom would know we barely spoke to each other that evening."

"Come on, no one will remember that. It was a New Year's Eve party. A lot of people were drinking."

"I wasn't," she pointed out.

"Well, of course you weren't."

"Hey—"

"I'm sure you never drink in public. Wouldn't suit the image of the judge, would it?"

Actually, she didn't drink out of fear of turning into her mother. But that certainly wasn't the kind of thing she wanted him to know.

"But even you," he continued, "as sober as you were, do you remember what every other person at the party was doing?"

Mostly she remembered the unending boredom of listening to Paul—Beth and Stew's accountant—describe his two-week glacier cruise to Alaska. But other than Paul, she couldn't remember how anyone else spent their evening. And despite how long it had felt, her conversation with Paul had lasted only twenty or so minutes.

"Okay, then," she conceded. "We 'fell in love' at the party. So we're set with a story."

"We need a few more details than that, don't you think?"

She let out a frustrated sigh. "What kind of details?"

"Well, if I remember right, it was a pretty warm night for December. We could say we went into the backyard to sit by the chiminea."

"That would explain why no one saw us together," she pointed out. Beth and Stew's house sat on more than half an acre of land. The long, narrow backyard was scattered with live oaks. For parties, Beth draped the limbs of the trees with lanterns. On a winter night, gathered around the warmth of the fire in the chiminea, it would be an undeniably romantic setting. The perfect place to fall in love.

"It does sound nice," she murmured. As soon as she heard how dreamy her tone sounded, she sat up straighter. "For the purposes of the story, I mean."

"Oh, of course. For the story."

He sounded amused. As if he sensed that she'd momentarily gotten caught up in the fake memory they were creating to pass off their fake marriage as real.

Part of her wished she could adopt a similarly cavalier attitude about the situation. But then, it was her job that was at stake, not his.

Which probably meant she should be more grateful that he'd come up with a story about how they'd fallen in love.

His attitude might seem cavalier, but he was taking their arrangement as seriously as she was. Maybe even more so.

"What about dating?" she asked, determined to do her part.

"What about it?"

"We certainly didn't go on any dates around town. Someone would have remembered that."

"Good point. I guess—" she heard a rustling of fabric in the background and for a second his voice was muffled "—we dated in Austin."

"We kept our relationship secret, though. Why would we do that?" she asked.

"I wanted to protect your reputation."

For some reason, that struck her as funny. So she was laughing as she replied, "That's awfully noble of you."

"What?" Mock offense laced his tone. "You don't think I'm noble?"

"Hey, you're marrying me to protect my reputation. I don't think it gets more noble than that."

"Right. Don't forget it, either."

"Don't worry. If you go through with this wedding, I'll really owe you one."

"Speaking of the wedding. I was, um—" he cleared his throat "—wondering what you wanted to do about the honeymoon."

"The honeymoon?" she finally choked out.

"Yeah. People will expect us to go away somewhere."

Dang. A honeymoon? Why hadn't she thought of that? And why, now that he'd mentioned it, did her mind suddenly fill with images of the two of them alone together in some romantic location. An exotic beach or quaint bed and breakfast.

"No," she said abruptly. "Absolutely not."

Letting her imagination run away with her was one

thing. Actually fulfilling one of those daydreams by letting Jake take her on a romantic getaway? That was out of the question.

He must have heard the pure horror in her voice, because he said, "Hey, it's not like I'd take you to the Bates Motel or anything. I was thinking something more along the lines of a B&B in Fredericksburg. Just for a night or two."

Right. A couple of nights in one of the most charming historic towns in Texas? She'd prefer the Bates Motel.

"No," she said firmly. "We're not going anywhere."

"But—"

"We're going to spend the weekend moving your stuff into my place like we discussed. We can tell people we're planning a big trip in the fall, if you want."

Before he could protest further, she said good-night and ended the call.

Five

"I can't believe you're doing this."

Beth sat in the spare chair in Kate's office. Her normally serene features were twisted into a frown, just as her hands were twisted into fretful knots where they lay on her lap.

Kate squelched her nerves and forced her attention back to her computer screen and the open document she'd been reading when Beth arrived at the courthouse a full hour early for the wedding.

"I know," Kate said, hoping to placate her sister's nerves. "I can hardly believe it myself."

"The thing is, Stew and I…" The tension in her voice drew Kate's gaze back to her. "Well, we never meant for this to happen. I mean, we knew we were asking a lot, but…"

With a sigh, Kate finally gave up on getting any more work done and closed the document on the screen. She rounded her desk to stand by Beth's chair. "I know you didn't. No one could have predicted things would turn out like this."

Beth looked up at her and Kate was surprised to see her sister's eyes brimming with tears. At the sight, the tension that had been building inside Kate over the past two weeks began to seep away.

"Hey." She leaned down and rubbed Beth's arm. "There's no need for tears. Everything's going to be fine."

Beth stood and clutched Kate's hands. "So you don't hate us?"

Kate hadn't realized it, but until that instant, she had been harboring some resentment.

Not for having to marry Jake. No, she blamed only herself for not realizing sooner the threat Hatcher posed to her career. But she did resent Beth because being pregnant had made Kate realize all that was missing from her life. Made her yearn for things she couldn't have, but that Beth could. But faced with Beth's obvious remorse, that, too, disappeared. "No," she reassured. "I don't hate you. How could I?"

"Because you…" Beth's voice broke. "You have to marry Jake. You hate Jake," she finished with a wail.

Even though there was nothing at all funny about the situation, Kate couldn't help chuckling. "I don't hate Jake." She glanced at the door to her office, verifying—again—that it was firmly closed.

"You were right about him, you know?" Kate admitted. "Jake is a really good guy."

More and more, Kate was realizing just how distorted her initial impression of Jake had been. When they first met at Beth and Stew's rehearsal dinner, she'd been put off by Jake's charm and good looks. She'd assumed they were all he had going for him. Funny, how wrong she'd been, when she was usually such a good judge of character. She couldn't think of any other man—not even Stew—who would marry a virtual stranger under such circumstances.

Beth smiled weakly. "He is a good guy, isn't he?"

"Absolutely. So you don't need to worry at all. Everything is going to turn out just fine." Kate smiled gamely and hoped it hid her own nerves. Despite her reassurances to Beth, she wasn't at all sure that everything would be anywhere near fine.

Beth must not have sensed any of the doubts plaguing Kate, because she offered a wobbly smile of her own.

"I brought you something. For the ceremony." She held up a brown paper shopping bag from her store the Health Nut. "I was hoping you'd wear it."

Kate felt a wave of sinking dread. "Oh, Beth…"

"I know you don't think of this as a real ceremony, but you should still have something nice to wear," Beth said in a rush. "It's not fancy. Not a real wedding dress or anything." She laughed nervously. "Not even I would bring you a real wedding dress in a grocery sack."

"I appreciate the offer, but I'm okay wearing what I have on."

"Please, Kate," Beth all but pleaded. "Let me do this. You never let me do anything nice for you."

"It's really not necessary."

"But I still hope you'll wear it. It would mean a lot to me."

Reluctantly Kate took the bag from her sister and pulled out the dress inside. It was a simple, cream-colored dress that would fall nearly to her ankles, with short cap sleeves and lace around the deep, heart-shaped neckline. Very feminine. Definitely the kind of thing she'd wear only to mollify her sister.

"I know it's not what you would usually wear," Beth began before Kate could protest. "But it matched the shawl."

With a sense of resignation, Kate reached back into the bag. She knew what she would find before her hand even touched it.

The delicate lace shawl that Beth had worn with her own wedding dress. The shawl that Stella—their adoptive mother—had worn with hers.

Shaking her head, she tried to hand the heirloom back to Beth. "I can't accept this."

But Beth refused to take the shawl, pressing it back into Kate's hands. "Stella would have wanted you to wear it."

No, Stella had wanted Beth to have it.

Kate and Stella had rarely gotten along during the nine years Kate lived with Stella and Dave—the adoptive parents that Beth adored and Kate could barely stand.

Before Kate could log any more protests, Beth squeezed her hand and said, "Please, do it for me. This way I'll know you've forgiven us."

How in the world was she supposed to say no to that?

"Besides," Beth added with a grin, "you can't wear what you have on. You look like a waiter."

Kate looked down at her outfit of wide-legged black crepe pants and tailored white shirt. "A waiter?"

So she caved. As she usually did when Beth looked at her with those big sad eyes. Funny, Beth was the older sister, yet Kate had always felt like the tough one. The one in control. The one who got things done and held things together.

Because she'd always been the tough one, she'd never been able to stand seeing Beth upset. Which—she admitted to herself as she was changing into the cream dress in the bathroom of the courthouse annex—was what had gotten her in this situation in the first place.

Just before sending Kate off to the bathroom to change, Beth had whipped out a brush and sparkly hair clip. She'd twisted and smoothed until Kate's scalp ached, forcing the black waves into some semblance of a style. Now, Kate smoothed the dress over her hips and eyed herself critically in the mirror. She was now fifteen weeks pregnant. The fabric clung a little snugly across her belly, but not noticeably so.

Never in a million years would she have picked this dress for herself. It was too frilly. Too girly. Exactly the kind of thing she thought she looked ridiculous in.

Kate looked longingly at her folded pants and shirt. Maybe she had resembled a waiter, but at least she'd looked like herself.

Now she looked like freakin' Snow White.

As she and Beth walked across the park to the main courthouse, she half expected birds and little woodland creatures to scurry to her side, chirping music.

Just outside the J.P.'s office, Kevin caught up with them.

"I'm sorry I'm la—" He cut himself off as he looked at Kate. "Whoa."

She glared back. "You're not late. And don't you dare say anything about how I'm dressed."

He held up his hands. "I was going to say you look great." He caught Beth's eye as he leaned in to brush a kiss hello on Kate's cheek. "This your idea?"

Beth smiled. "Absolutely."

He smiled. "I heartily approve."

Kate narrowed her gaze. "You are worthless as a best friend. First you're late and now this?"

She reached for the handle of the door to the J.P.'s office, but Beth plastered herself against the solid wood.

"Hold on, you can't go in there."

"What? Why not?"

Beth clucked disapprovingly. "Because they might not be ready for you. You can't go in until they are, otherwise the groom will see you before the wedding and that will be bad luck." Beth cracked open the door and peeked inside. "Jake and Stew are already inside. I'll just check on things."

Kate opened her mouth to protest, but snapped it closed when Kevin caught her eye.

In front of him, she couldn't point out that it hardly mattered if Jake saw her before he wedding, because this wasn't a real wedding. So she kept her mouth shut, fumed silently and tried to ignore the satisfied smile Kevin was bestowing on her.

After several moments, she gave in to her curiosity and demanded, "What?"

"What?" he parroted.

"You're looking entirely too smug. Why?"

"I don't know what you mean." He smiled innocently.

"I hope you don't have anything silly planned because—"

Before she could finish with her threat to make his life miserable, Beth opened the door to the J.P.'s office, revealing exactly why Kevin looked so smug.

Kate had expected to see five people at most inside Judge Walthen's chambers. Instead, dozens of people were crammed into the already small room. Judge Walthen stood behind his desk, which had been cleared to make room for several large vases of day lilies. Her favorite. To Walthen's left, stood Jake—looking so breathtakingly handsome that he…well, he took her breath away.

She hadn't seen Jake in a suit since Beth and Stew's wedding. The crisp white shirt showed off the tanned column of his throat. And his broad shoulders did things for a suit jacket that should be illegal.

But it was his expression that stopped her in her tracks. As he turned to face her, the cocky grin he usually wore faded, replaced by delight as he studied her.

She couldn't help feeling a bubble of feminine pleasure at the appreciative gleam in his eyes. For a second he looked almost like a man in love.

Then he ruined the effect by flashing her a grin accompanied by a quick wink.

And just like that, the bubble of pleasure she'd felt popped.

To him this was all a joke. To her, it was little more than an obligation. A trial to be endured. Not a celebration.

As for the friends who had shown up for the wedding…she was deceiving them. And she'd continue to deceive them for as long as it took to keep her job.

Suddenly it felt right that Beth had forced her into this frilly dress and heirloom shawl. It was the perfect costume for this farce. She was little more than an actress who'd wandered onto stage during a play. Except she didn't know which play she was in and she certainly didn't know any of her lines.

Nevertheless, she forced herself to put one foot in front of the other, and by the time she reached Jake's side, her uncertainty had crystallized into anger. This was all his fault.

The flowers, the guests—none of this could have been done without his knowledge. Surely he could have guessed she wouldn't have wanted any of this.

He leaned over to brush a kiss against her cheek and whispered, "Smile. No one will buy this if you keep looking like you want to kill me."

He pulled back and took her hand in his. Knowing he

was right, she plastered a smile onto her lips that she hoped passed for either "nervous bride" or "dopey romantic."

She could kill him later.

"I now pronounce you husband and wife."

Kate's hand felt clammy in his. At least, she no longer looked ready to faint. Or strangle him.

Her expression remained strained, but most people would probably write that off as nerves. Which would be normal, under the circumstances. He didn't know how men did this for real. Hell, he'd been a nervous wreck all day.

Except for the moment when he'd turned to see Kate standing in the doorway. In that instant everything felt right. Alarmingly so.

But he'd shoved the sensation aside. Just as he'd done with the well of emotion he felt while sliding the simple platinum wedding band onto her finger.

Whatever he'd felt, surely it wasn't pleasure. Pride, maybe, in living up to his responsibilities. Doing the right thing.

Satisfied that he'd pigeonholed his feelings, he returned his attention to the judge just in time to hear the words, "You may now kiss the bride."

A glance in the direction of the audience revealed a sea of expectant faces. Kate, on the other hand, looked as if she was wavering between feeling faint and wanting to stomp on his foot with the heel of her shoe.

But whether she liked it or not, he had to kiss her.

For a second he merely stared down into her wide brown eyes. Her lips were parted slightly and moist, because she'd licked them nervously during the ceremony.

Kissing Kate would be no hardship.

Part of him had been thinking about this moment ever

since he'd first agreed to marry her—maybe longer. His first kiss with Kate.

Maybe his only kiss with her.

He felt a surge of anticipation mixed with determination. If this was going to be their only kiss, then he was going to make it count. Why the hell not? She already wanted to kill him anyway.

So he wrapped one arm around her shoulders to pull her toward him and with the other hand he tilted up her chin in the instant before his lips came to rest on hers, he caught a 'Don't you dare' expression in her eyes. But he did dare.

Her mouth was soft and pliant beneath his. From surprise, most likely. Because as soon as she realized he wasn't pulling away immediately, her lips stiffened and her hands pressed into his chest. She could easily have pushed him away if she'd really wanted to, but she never quite mustered the resistance.

At the feel of her lips beneath his, the taste of her on his mouth, desire sprung to life, pumping through his blood. He found himself aching to press her against his body, to deepen the kiss. He barely restrained himself from sweeping his tongue into her mouth.

But he did manage to finally pull back. He didn't want her like this—kissing him because she had to. He wanted her eager. Warm and pliant. Hell, he just wanted her.

He nearly cursed as he let her go. Because his new wife was the one woman he couldn't have.

Six

"This isn't what we talked about," Kate muttered through clenched teeth forty minutes later as they stood in the private dining room of the 7th Street Bistro. The bistro was one of the trendy new restaurants that had opened on the square across from the courthouse.

Tonight the private room was filled with the guests who had come to help them celebrate. Champagne toasts were being made to their happiness. Large platters of appetizers were being passed around.

Jake held a glass of champagne in one hand but kept his other arm draped over Kate's shoulder, partly for appearance's sake and partly to keep her by his side. The minute he let go, he knew she'd pull away from him.

"I hope this wasn't your idea," she said under her breath.

He'd guided her to the back of the room by a table laden with a two-tier cake and a dozen or so packages wrapped in shades of white paper. They stood slightly apart from the crowd, so there was no chance of being overheard. But they were being closely watched.

"Not a chance." He leaned in to brush a kiss on her temple and caught the scent of her shampoo. Something sweet and fruity. Damn, she smelled good.

She nudged her shoulder against his chest. "Stop doing that," she hissed.

"What?"

"Being all lovey-dovey. It's ridiculous."

"This is our wedding reception," he pointed out. "It'd be ridiculous if we *weren't* affectionate."

She made a disgruntled noise. "So, if this wasn't your idea, then whose was it?"

"Your friend Kevin. He's the one responsible." Just then Kevin caught his eye from across the room and smiled broadly. Not wanting to spoil the guy's fun, Jake raised his glass in salute before downing a healthy gulp.

"I'm going to kill him," she muttered. "When this is over, I'm definitely going to kill him."

"He just wanted to do something nice for you. Why is that so hard for you to accept?"

He studied her, genuinely curious about her reaction

"Nice?" Kate scoffed. "Nice would have been arranging for me to have the afternoon off. This is torture."

"Ah, it's not so bad."

"Not so bad? Half the town is here."

"Thirty people is hardly half the town." She merely glared at him, so he added, "Try to look on the bright side—"

"The bright side?" she asked sarcastically before he could finish.

He ignored her. "At least now everyone knows about the wedding. That was the idea, wasn't it?"

Turning to face him, she said, "Speaking of things

people know about. All of this might not have been your idea, but you knew about it, didn't you?"

He could lie, but what would be the point? "As soon as Kevin found out we were getting married, he started planning this. I found out on…oh, about Tuesday, I guess."

"And you didn't put a stop to it?"

"Don't you think that would have seemed strange? Besides, what's the harm?"

"What's the harm?" she asked incredulously. "If we're not careful—if we slip up at all, any one of these people could put two and two together and figure out that we barely know each other. And that we're certainly not in love."

"That's not going to happen."

"How can you be so sure?"

He nodded toward the room. "Look at them. Do any of them look suspicious? Even a little bit?"

She twisted to study the crowd, carefully examining each face. He allowed her a few seconds of paranoia before nudging her chin with his knuckle so she looked back at him. "The only thing that might make people suspicious is if we don't act like happy newlyweds."

Her mouth opened and closed several times as if she were considering a protest. Finally she snapped her mouth shut and just glared at him. She looked so damn cute when she was mad, he simply couldn't resist kissing her petulant lips.

Unlike the kiss after the ceremony, this time, she didn't put up much resistance. Too surprised, he supposed. Her lips parted beneath his almost instantly, and with one quick swipe of his tongue he felt her defiance give way completely.

She tasted just faintly of champagne.

When they first arrived at the reception, someone

had thrust a flute into her hand, and ever since then she'd been dutifully raising it to her mouth with every toast. Thankfully, no one else noticed the glass was full. Still, a few drops of the champagne clung to her lips.

The taste, so unexpected and sweet, surprised him. Just like she did.

He pulled back from her and studied her face. For a second she looked slightly shell-shocked. He suspected he did, too.

Then she shook it off and said, "Why did you do that?"

"Kiss you?"

She nodded.

"Because, we just got married. There are thirty people in this room who think we're so in love we couldn't wait long enough to plan a church wedding. Therefore, I should look like I can't keep my hands off you."

Doubt flickered in her eyes and for a second, he thought she wasn't going to buy it. Finally she nodded. And with an expression of resigned determination, she slipped her arm around his waist and turned to face the crowded room, where the wait staff was just beginning to serve an early dinner.

He felt a surge of relief that she hadn't pressed him for another explanation. Sure, the one he'd given her worked, but it wasn't the whole truth.

Just now he'd kissed her because he wanted to. The ruse they were perpetrating hadn't even entered his mind.

He was in for a hell of a long six months.

Kate awakened to the unfamiliar sounds of someone moving around in her kitchen. After a split second of alarm, she remembered that someone was Jake.

With a groan she rolled over and buried her head in

her pillow, wishing she could go back to sleep. Or wake up to find she'd just had a nightmare.

She'd lain awake half the night, trying to find fault with Jake's logic. But no matter how she approached the problem, his solution was the only one. Whenever they were in public, they'd have to appear to be in love. Which meant more touches, more kisses and more restless nights knowing he was sleeping just a few feet away in her tiny bungalow-style house's only other bedroom.

After a few more seconds of squeezing her eyes closed, she sat up to face another morning without coffee. Boy, could she have used the caffeine this morning. At least her morning sickness had finally passed.

She had her arms halfway into the sleeves of her robe before it occurred to her that she really didn't want Jake seeing her in her pj's and robe. There was way too much intimacy between them as it was.

So she took the time to dress in a casual pair of pants and long sleeved shirt that she knotted low on her waist to distract from the slight bulge. Then she made a quick trip to the bathroom to twist her unruly hair into a semblance of an elegant knot and to run a toothbrush over her teeth.

She found Jake in the kitchen, barefoot, dressed in jeans and a faded black T-shirt, scrambling eggs. Lots of eggs.

When she cleared her throat, he glanced over his shoulder. "Mornin', Katie."

Letting the annoying nickname slide, she said, "I don't know what pregnancy books you've been reading, but although pregnant women do eat a lot, they generally don't eat two dozen eggs for breakfast."

He chuckled. "God, I hope not. I couldn't afford to feed you. These are for the guys. Besides, it's not just eggs, it's breakfast tacos." He lifted the spatula from the frying pan and pointed toward the oven. "The first batch is in the oven. Help yourself."

"Breakfast tacos?" she repeated dreamily. In her mind, nothing beat the sheer joy from consuming eggs, bacon, melted Colby-jack and spicy salsa all wrapped up in a warm tortilla.

"Yep. Those are bacon, egg and cheese. These'll be sausage, egg, and potato, if you want to wait. And there's decaf coffee in the pot."

She was already fishing a couple of tacos out of the oven when he got to the part about the coffee. "Decaf? Is that what you normally drink?"

"Naw. Normally, I'm a double-shot espresso kinda guy. But Beth mentioned you'd given up caffeine. I figured, if you could do it, so could I."

"My gosh, you're a saint for giving up coffee if you don't have to." She dropped the tacos onto a plate and began gingerly peeling away the hot tinfoil he'd wrapped them in. "Where'd you get all this food? I could have sworn I didn't have five dozen eggs in the fridge."

"I went out to the store this morning."

She glanced at the clock. "It's only 8:30. How long have you been up?"

"Let's just say that inflatable mattress you blew up for me last night wasn't quite made for someone my size."

"Ah. Sorry. Not having a proper guest bed means unwanted guests don't stay for long. Sorry you had to pay the price though. On the bright side, it does give us an excuse to move your bed and furniture into my guest bedroom."

There hadn't been time before their wedding night to move in his bed. Which had left either the sofa or the inflatable mattress. "By the way, when you said these were for 'the guys' which 'guys' did you mean exactly?"

"The guys from the station." He dumped the scrambled eggs into the bowl of already cooked sausage and potatoes.

"Just so I know what to expect—" she spooned salsa onto her tacos "—will 'the guys' be coming over every Saturday morning for breakfast?"

"No."

"Oh, that's good."

She'd been teasing, but as she took a bike of taco, it occurred to her: What did she really know about Jake, other than the fact that he was an arson investigator and had been Stew's best friend since the tenth grade? And he made kick-butt breakfast tacos.

Everything else was supposition and extrapolation. And yet she'd invited him into her home—into her life—for the next six months. What in the world had she gotten herself into?

And did it really matter as long as he kept feeding her like this? she mused as she took another bite of taco.

With her foot she nudged a kitchen chair away from the table so it faced the counter where Jake worked. She lowered herself into the chair, held a napkin under her chin so she didn't drip on her shirt and took another bite.

Man, oh, man, she could get used to this.

Freshly made breakfast tacos. Hot coffee waiting for her. Jake sure knew the way to a woman's heart.

"The guys are helping to move my stuff in. I offered to feed them as payment." As he stirred the ingredients together, he studied her over his shoulder. "I told them—"

She looked at him over her taco. "What?"

"That's what you're wearing?" His eyebrows were raised, his expression dubious.

She glanced down, just to verify that her pants and shirt hadn't somehow morphed into a Big Bird costume. "What's wrong with what I have on?"

He looked her up and down with a thoroughness she found more than a little disconcerting. "Nothing. I guess."

She looked down at her clothes again, then back up at him. "Seriously, what's wrong with this?"

He shrugged, turning his attention back to filling the tortillas. "It's just a little formal for a Saturday morning, don't you think?"

"No, obviously I didn't think so or I wouldn't have put it on." She frowned at his back and added wryly, "But compared to your jeans and ratty T-shirt, I guess I am dressed somewhat formally."

He gave her a cocky grin over his shoulder. "Hey, it's moving day. Jeans and a ratty T-shirt are perfect."

"Yes, well, I don't have any jeans," she mumbled around a mouthful of taco.

He stilled instantly, then slowly turned to face her, an expression of mock horror on his face. "You don't own any jeans?"

She lifted her chin defiantly and met his gaze. "No, I don't."

"You don't own jeans," he repeated. "That's the damnedest thing I've ever heard. Why don't you own jeans? I'm only asking 'cause you must be the only person in the U.S. under the age of ninety who doesn't."

For a moment she gritted her teeth, then finally admitted, "If you must know, jeans don't flatter my particular body shape."

He let out a bark of laughter. "That's the stupidest thing I've ever heard."

"It's not stu—"

But he was laughing too hard for her to finish.

"What? You think they make your butt look too big or something?" When she didn't answer, he stopped laughing and studied her. "That's it, isn't it? You think jeans make your butt look big."

"I'm not even going to dignify that with a response."

He looked her up and down appreciatively. "You don't have to, 'cause I know I'm right. But let me put your mind at ease, Katie. Your butt is most definitely not too big."

She clenched and unclenched her jaw, unsure what annoyed her more: his use of the nickname Katie or the way his lingering gaze made her breath catch in her chest.

Finally she choked out the only response she could muster without embarrassing herself further. "My butt is not too big. I'll have you know that according to the current standards of the Surgeon General's Office, my pre-pregnancy weight was perfectly in line for someone my height and age."

He nodded, smiling. "Well, it's good to know the surgeon general and I agree. Now that we've got that settled, we need to do something about your clothes."

She looked down at herself again. "Isn't that what we've been talking about? Since I don't have any jeans, I don't see that there's much we can do about it."

He propped his hip against the counter and studied her with his arms crossed over his chest. "No, you're right. But it's not so much your clothes as it is your general appearance."

"Now you're insulting my 'general appearance'? What's next—my personal hygiene? My politics?"

He stroked his chin, seemingly unaware of how insulting this all was. "It's not that there's anything wrong with your appearance per se. It's that you don't look particularly…satisfied."

Humph. What was that supposed to mean?

She crossed her arms over her chest and glared at him. "Well, I'll certainly look a lot less dissatisfied if you stop insulting me."

He pushed away from the countertop and crossed the kitchen to stand before her, all the while sporting one of his arrogant grins. "Oh, I think we can do a lot better than 'less dissatisfied.'"

With him standing over her as she sat, he had her at a distinct disadvantage. So she bumped her chair back and stood. Unfortunately, that only brought her closer to him.

But she refused to be intimidated by his height. Or his nearness. Or the delectable way he smelled—like coffee and bacon and freshly showered man.

"I'll have you know, I think there's nothing wrong with my appearance."

His lips twitched in a way she was sure he knew irritated her. "Sure, if we were just going to hang out here all morning by ourselves, but…"

"But?" She arched an eyebrow.

"But the guys from the station are coming over."

"I've appeared in court like this." She propped her hands on her hips. "I certainly think this will do for your friends from the station."

He continued to study her, he scratched the back of his head as if he was trying to solve a very complex puzzle. "Well, there you go. That's the problem. You look like you're going to court."

"And that's a problem because…"

"Because you should look like you just tumbled out of bed."

Her heart seemed to skip a beat at his words. She sucked in a deep breath, but the extra oxygen didn't counteract what had to be some kind of weird prenatal heart arrhythmia.

She opened her mouth to speak, but all that came out was a weak, "I… I…"

"The way I see it, the morning after her wedding night, a woman ought to look thoroughly…"

Before she could stop herself, the words just popped out. "Thoroughly made love to?"

A wicked gleam sparked in his eyes. "I was going to say satisfied."

"Oh." She could feel a blush creeping into her cheeks and she floundered for a moment. "I, um…"

There were moments in life when she wished she was a completely different person. Someone witty and quick, instead of smart and serious. This was definitely one of those moments.

Another woman might have thought of something clever to say that would have put Jake in his place. Or shocked him into silence. She merely stood there, gaping like a trout.

In this game of witty repartee, it was Jake one, Kate big fate zero.

"Obviously, we need to start with this," he said, reaching up and pulling the clip from her elegant knot.

Her hair fell down about her neck as she heard the clip land on the table beside her with a clatter.

"Now it probably looks like I just tumbled out of bed." She grumbled in protest.

He grinned. "That's the general idea."

Instantly she brought one hand up to smooth her hair into place and reached for the clip with the other. Before she could repair the damage, he grabbed her arm by the wrist and tugged it away from her hair.

"Let me."

Let him what?

But before she could demand an answer, he finger combed her hair, gently parting it on the left.

Stop this! she ordered herself. But she didn't listen. His touch simply felt too good. Her eyes drifted closed.

"Your hair is beautiful. You should wear it loose more often."

"It gets frizzy," she said weakly. "In the humidity. And it doesn't do what I want it to. Looks uncontrollable."

"Wild?"

His voice was like a caress. Sensuous and a little rough. It sapped her strength and when she spoke her voice sounded weak.

"Yes."

"And you don't like that," he surmised.

"No."

"Being wild isn't such a bad thing. It's sexy."

Like Jake. He always seemed so wild. So reckless.

Well, her hair might be wild, but *she* definitely wasn't.

She forced her eyes open. Forced herself to meet his gaze and to suppress the wave of longing she felt rising up inside of her.

There was heat in his gaze, as well. Proof that this crazy awareness she felt wasn't one-sided. But wanting Jake would do no good. And giving in to the want would only cause more problems than she could imagine.

Yet before she could force herself to move away from him, he pulled his hands from her hair, only to lower them to the top button of her shirt.

"This shirt here. That's another problem." His voice was low and rough and grated against her already-sensitive nerves.

"It is?"

"Definitely." His fingers slipped first one and then

another button loose from its hole. His knuckles brushed against the sensitive skin of her throat and chest, sending flashes of heat spiraling down through her body.

She felt herself swaying toward him, suddenly unable to control her own body. Even though she knew what a mistake it would be, she found herself mentally urging him to keep unbuttoning. To pull her shirt right off her.

He must have had way more restraint than she did in that instant, because instead of ripping her shirt open, his hands dropped to where she'd knotted the hem of her shirt low on her hips. Patiently he loosened the knot.

She sucked in her breath as the tail of her shirt fell from his hands and his fingers continued unbuttoning.

With every movement of his fingers, she willed him to meet her eyes, desperate to see his expression. But he kept his attention focused on the task he performed with such painstaking gentleness.

By the time he retied the tail of her shirt into a loose knot just under her breasts, she felt light-headed and weak. In undoing the buttons on her shirt, he'd stripped away all of her defenses, as well.

Still, when he stepped back to eye his handiwork, her hands darted to the skin he'd exposed. He grabbed her wrists before she could cover herself.

"Don't."

"But my stomach is so much rounder than—"

"Leave it." Finally his gaze met hers and he seemed completely serious for the first time since they'd met. "You look…fantastic."

The doorbell rang. Jake dropped his hands to his sides. They both stared toward the front door.

She could hardly bear the intrusion. The reminder of how little this encounter must have meant to Jake.

After all, the past few minutes had been little more than skillful manipulation. When he'd said she looked "fantastic," what he'd really meant was that she looked "satisfied." Like a woman who'd just been made love to. Like the woman his friends expected to see.

As Jake moved to get the door, she snatched the clip from the table and quickly twisted her hair back into a knot. But of course, it was too late. Before she could repair the damage and redo the buttons on her shirt, Jake's friends were pouring through the front door.

They'd seen her hastily putting herself back together. The way their voices, one by one, dropped, from loud, rambunctious chatter into silence proved at least that much.

A scorching heat crept up her neck into her cheeks, fueled by embarrassment and kindled with more than a little anger. Anger at Jake for manipulating her, but mostly anger at herself for falling so completely under his spell.

She knew better, damn it.

At least, she thought she did.

What was the point of carefully constructing defenses against men, if she cheerfully threw open the gates and allowed in the first man with a charming smile and plateful of breakfast tacos.

Man, she was easy—when she looked at it in that light.

Jake had been in her home less than a day, and she'd melted like an ice cube. And to think, while he'd been plying her with tacos, she'd been telling herself how she could get used to this.

As Jake's friends flooded the kitchen and began fixing plates, pouring coffee and introducing themselves, she felt her determination hardening.

She might not be able to control her physical reaction to Jake, but, by golly, she was going to control her emotions. Make herself less susceptible to him. Which meant no more decaf coffee. No more hot breakfasts. No more morning intimacies. She was not going to "get used to this." Not if she could help it.

At least Jake's friends were polite enough not to say anything about what they'd seen, but their sideways glances and knowing grins said plenty. They'd inferred exactly what Jake meant for them to.

They assumed she and Jake had spent their wedding night the traditional way. Making passionate love.

Funny, she'd never felt less satisfied.

Seven

In the month since their marriage, Kate had certainly kept her distance.

She worked long hours, which Jake, of course, had expected. She went to the gym almost every day for prenatal workout and yoga classes. And when she was home, she spent most of her time in her room, "resting," she claimed, which made sense, because he knew pregnant women needed lots of sleep.

All of that he could put up with. If only she'd let him help her. With anything. But she wasn't letting him.

He'd offered to help with her laundry. She'd refused and started sending it out to be done. He'd tried to cook dinner for her in the evenings. She insisted on eating microwaved frozen meals. Every morning he had a pot of hot decaf brewing by the time she emerged from her bedroom fully dressed. And every morning she walked right past it on her way out the door to Starbucks.

Yes, he'd pushed too hard the morning the guys from that station came over. He knew that now. For the life of him, he couldn't explain why he'd pushed at all. All he knew was that when Kate entered the kitchen dressed so primly, he hadn't been able to resist trying to ruffle her a bit. Maybe because he remembered how good she'd felt in his arms when they'd kissed. Or because he didn't like the thought of her coming to breakfast dressed so formally every morning for the next six months. Or maybe he'd just wanted to kiss her again and couldn't resist finding out whether she wanted that, too.

Frankly, he didn't know what to do anymore.

Which was why, one Thursday night after work, instead of heading home, he stopped by Beth's and Stew's to get their advice.

"We haven't seen you in a while," Stew said as he flipped a vegetarian hamburger on the grill in the backyard.

"If I'd known you were making burgers, I would have gotten here early enough to claim one."

Stew laughed. "You're welcome to one. But only one." With his spatula he gestured to the three burgers sizzling on the grill. "There's no way I'm taking food out of the mouth of a pregnant woman. You know what I mean?"

Jake chuckled and nodded. But the truth was, he didn't know what Stew meant. That was the problem. That was why he'd come here this evening for Stew's advice.

Carrying buttered hamburger buns for Stew to grill, Beth greeted Jake warmly, as she always did. He couldn't help noticing her clothes. Sure, she was a full month farther along than Kate, but Beth was already wearing in long, flowing maternity dresses, designed to show off her belly. Kate, on the other hand, was still dressing to hide her pregnancy. Something she wouldn't be able to get away with for much longer.

Beth set the buns down by the grill, then shot a pointed look at Stew. Not too subtle.

Especially when Stew cleared his throat a few seconds later and asked, "So how's Kate doing?"

Funny, he'd been about to ask them the same question. But apparently Stew and Beth didn't know any more than he did. "Okay. I think." He ran his hand down the back of his neck. "Has she always been so…"

He wasn't sure exactly how to finish the thought tactfully.

"Difficult?" Beth piped up.

"Closed off?" Stew supplied.

"I was going to say 'unwilling to accept help.'"

Beth nodded. "Yep, that's Kate for you. She's always needed to do things her own way. Frankly, it'd be annoying, if she wasn't usually right."

"She won't let me do anything for her. It's driving me crazy," he admitted.

Stew chuckled.

"What?" Jake shot an annoyed look at his friend.

"Man, this must be killing you."

"What's that supposed to mean?"

"Well…you know how you are."

"No." He gritted his teeth. "Apparently, I don't know."

"You need to save people. Be the hero."

"I need to save people?" Jake repeated. Then he scoffed at the idea. "I don't need to save people. That's ridiculous."

Stew and Beth gave each other an amused look.

"I don't need to save people."

Stew used his spatula to transfer the burgers from the grill to the waiting plate. "Sure you do. It's why you became a firefighter. It's why you agreed to marry Kate. It's—"

"I agreed to marry Kate because it was the right thing to do. She needed a husband and she needed someone to take care of her while she's pregnant."

"Right," Stew said. "And you want to be the one who takes care of her, because you need to save people. It's not a bad thing."

"It does explain why you're having so many problems with Kate," Beth said. "She doesn't need anyone to save her. She hasn't since she was a little girl. She doesn't need anyone, period."

And that—Jake realized as he drove home later that night—was the crux of the problem. Kate didn't need anyone's help. Not even his.

Maybe Stew was right and he did need to be a hero, because it drove him crazy that Kate didn't need him.

In some ways, the realization relieved the tension that had been eating away at him the past month. Kate had been getting to him. After all, she was a beautiful woman and they were living together. The physical attraction he felt for her was only natural.

But this was more than purely sexual. He thought about her all the time and had to resist the urge to call her at work. Just to check in.

He thought about ways to tease her. Things he could say just to get a rise out of her.

His growing attachment to her had become quite a problem.

But now…now he had a clue what was really going on. Stew was right. He needed to be a hero.

He'd married Kate so he could help her, and she wasn't letting him. All he had to do was get her to accept his help and—presto—his Kate obsession would disappear.

* * *

He crept into the house a little after eleven, expecting Kate to be in bed already. So he was pretty damn surprised to find her stretched out on the sofa, remote control in hand, a late-night rerun of a crime drama on TV.

She slept through him turning off the TV and pulling the remote from her hand, but woke when he tried to cover her with the throw from the back of the sofa.

"You're home." She wiped at her eyes with her fingertips as she sat up. She looked delightfully sleepy, mussed by her nap. She was dressed in baggy pajamas. Pink with fat ladybugs scattered across them. He'd never seen her in her pajamas before, since she always dressed before leaving her bedroom.

For that matter he hadn't seen her barefoot since that first morning. He glanced down at her feet. Sure enough, they were bare. Slim with high arches and red-painted toenails. Ladybug-red.

He never would have guessed her for red toenails.

She must have caught him looking at her feet, because she quickly hid them as she sat cross-legged on the sofa.

He forced his gaze back to her face. "You didn't have to wait up."

"I wasn't. I just—" She frowned and glanced toward the TV. "What time is it, anyway?"

"About eleven-thirty."

"That late?"

He wasn't sure if the hint of accusation he heard in her voice was real or a figment of his guilt. Either way, his knee-jerk reaction was defensive. "I called."

"I know. But you shouldn't feel like you have to report in. You can stay out as late as you want."

Having apparently said what she'd needed to say, she

unfolded herself from the sofa and stood. Only as she was headed toward the hall did he notice how tired she looked.

"If you weren't waiting up for me, why were you sleeping on the sofa?"

She hesitated in the doorway to the hall, and for a second he thought she'd just ignore his question altogether. Then she turned to face him, propping her shoulder against the door frame. "Insomnia."

Her arms were crossed over her chest in a defensive posture. Waiting for him to tease her, he supposed. She looked cute, standing there in her ladybug pj's and bare feet. Vulnerable in a way she almost never was. And that appealed to him.

Not that he wanted her to be weak. He just wanted her to let him in occasionally.

"Insomnia, huh?" he prodded, willing her to say more.

"I've had it on and off for years. Mostly on. I can usually cope with it pretty well."

"And sleeping on the sofa helps?" he asked doubtfully.

"A little. The doctor said I shouldn't sleep on my back. Apparently it restricts the flow of blood to the placenta. So, when I do fall asleep, every time I roll over, I wake up, afraid I've rolled onto my back. At least on the sofa there's nowhere to roll. But it's less comfortable, so I still have trouble falling asleep. Unfortunately, a lot of the things I usually do to relax, you can't do when you're pregnant."

"Like drinking a glass of wine?"

She smiled. "I was thinking more along the lines of taking a hot bath. That usually helped. But I'm not supposed to raise my body temperature above 102 degrees. So the hot bath is out."

Into his mind popped an image of her soaking in the bathtub, surrounded by bubbles, hair piled high on her head, skin silky and moist, gleaming in the flickering light from a nearby candle.

He shoved the image aside and cleared his throat. This was not the time to be fantasizing about Kate. That tended to lead to wanting Kate. And wanting Kate was what had scared her off the last time.

Now that she'd finally started to relax around him again, he didn't want to screw this up. He wanted to do the right thing. To be helpful, damn it.

"There's gotta be something you can do to help you relax enough to sleep. Back when I was fighting fires, I'd come home from the job all keyed up from the adrenaline. I wouldn't be able to sleep."

Her lips curved into one of her rare smiles. "Well, I did blow out a candle earlier. But that's hardly the same thing."

He smiled. "You're into the second trimester, right?"

"This is my nineteenth week, so yeah."

"Isn't that when women are supposed to feel all energetic? Clean a lot or something?"

"Right. Nesting. It's when women are supposed to go through the nesting stage."

"Exactly. Tonight when I saw Stew, he said Beth was driving him crazy. She'd reorganized every closet in the house and was having him paint everything that stood still."

She laughed. "I guess that explains why I got a message from her last week wanting to go through some old stuff of our adopted Mom's."

"So you're probably nesting, too. That's why you have so much extra energy."

"Right." Her smile faded. "Except, I have no nest. I mean, sure, I've got a house I could clean and paint and organize, but what's the point, really? I don't have a baby to get ready for."

Her tone sounded almost wistful, and before he could stop himself, he asked, "Having second thoughts?"

Her gaze darted to his. "About?"

"Do you want to keep the baby?"

"No." She shook her head. "Absolutely not," she said a bit too firmly. After a second she looked at him curiously. "You're not…"

"Not what?"

"Thinking *you* want to keep the baby, are you?"

"No. God, no." But even as he said the words he knew they weren't entirely true. Of course he'd thought about it. But what could a guy like him offer a kid that Beth and Stew couldn't? He took a moment to study Kate and he asked, "You're sure you're not—"

"Definitely sure."

"Good."

"Right." She nodded. But then she tilted her head to the side and studied him. "I know Beth and Stew have said they want us to at least consider it, but as far as I'm concerned, it's not even an option."

It wasn't any of his business, but he couldn't help saying, "Okay, I know why I'm not even considering it. I know how my own dad struggled to raise me alone. But what about you? Why are you so dead set against it?"

She shrugged. "Some women are mommy material. Some aren't."

"And you think you aren't?" he asked, because she sounded a little too sure of her answer. Who was she trying to convince? Him or herself?

"Isn't that rather obvious?" She didn't wait for him to answer, but shifted the conversation back to their previous topic. "I see your point about the nesting, though." Words poured out of her. It was her avoidance technique, he was beginning to recognize. Anything she didn't want to think about, she just talked through. "Let's face it, sitting on the bench all day isn't exactly a high-energy job. I guess I could use some of that nesting energy to do some reorganizing around here—"

She broke off when he chuckled.

Narrowing her gaze, she demanded, "What?"

He looked pointedly around the living room, gesturing to the perfectly fluffed pillows, the neat fan of this month's magazines and the woven basket that held the TV remotes. "I'm just wondering what exactly you'd organize. Maybe rearrange the DVDs by genre before alphabetizing them? Group the candles on the mantel by height instead of color?"

Her gaze got even squintier and he couldn't tell if she was annoyed with his teasing or trying not to laugh.

"Ah, come on, Katie, even you have to admit there's not a lot around here that needs organization."

She shrugged, pushed herself away from the doorjamb and moved toward him. "So, back when you were fighting fires, what did you do to relax? Besides get drunk and take bubble baths, I mean."

"Firefighters don't take bubble baths."

"That's a shame. You tough guys are really missing out on one of life's great pleasures."

Kate naked in a bathtub? Oh, man. One of life's great pleasures indeed.

He felt heat beginning to creep up the back of his neck just thinking about it. Man, he needed to change the subject. "I…um…"

Kate let out a bark of laughter. "I've embarrassed you."

"No, I—"

"I have, haven't I? Look at that—" she gestured toward his face "—you're blushing."

He was blushing?

He was really in trouble now. He certainly couldn't tell her that he wasn't blushing, just hot under the collar from thinking about her.

"I…um…" He fumbled for a suitable lie, but came up with nothing.

"Don't worry," she said, chuckling. "I won't tell anyone that the big tough arson investigator embarrasses so easily. And just at the thought of taking a bath. That's pretty funny." She cocked her head to the side as if something just occurred to her. "Unless it's because you really do take bubble baths."

"I don't take bubble baths."

"That must be it. You take bubble baths."

"I don't. Trust me."

"Okay." But her smug grin told him she didn't believe him at all.

"I don't," he insisted through gritted teeth.

"I believe you." She slanted him a mischievous look. "But just in case you're lying, don't worry. Your secret is safe with me."

He opened his mouth to respond, only to snap it shut again, his rebuttal left unsaid. Unless he really did want to tell her what he'd been thinking about, there was no point in protesting.

Still grinning like she knew his deepest secret, she said, "So, besides taking bubble baths, what do big tough firefighters do to relax after a fire?"

For him, the best way to come down off an adrenaline rush had always been sex. The release that came with a couple of hot sweaty hours in bed had always done the trick.

Of course, he hadn't always been in a position to use that form of relaxation. He was too smart to risk casual sex in this day and age. A trip to the local dive with the other guys was always his second choice. He'd never needed a third. Until now.

Now, he racked his brain trying to think of a suggestion.

"What about exercise?" he tossed out.

"Why do you think I've been going to the gym five times a week?"

"Not working, huh?"

"It helps me fall asleep, but inevitably I wake up after a couple of hours and I just can't get comfortable again. I usually end up out here on the sofa."

"With the TV on?"

"Usually."

"I can't believe that doesn't wake me up."

"I hate to break it to you, but you sleep like the dead."

"Must be my mattress. Anyone would sleep like the dead on it. It's one of those adjustable air-filled ones. It's really—" He grinned, suddenly remembering a childhood remedy for sleeplessness. "I've got it."

"Got what?"

"The trick to help you fall back asleep." He grabbed her hand and pulled her into the kitchen.

"What? You're going to feed me?"

"Better. I'm going to make you warm milk."

"Warm milk?" She stuck her tongue out. "Bleck."

He pulled out one of the chairs from the table and nudged her toward it. "Have you ever tried it?"

"No," she admitted.

"Trust me. You'll love it."

She crossed her arms over her chest. "It sounds gross."

He pulled a saucepan out of a cabinet and the milk from the fridge. "My mother used to swear by this stuff. She made it for me all the time when I was little." He poured about a cup of milk into the pan and cranked up the heat on the burner.

A few minutes later as the milk came to a simmer, he pulled the pot from the stove and poured the liquid into a mug. He brought the mug to where Kate was sitting at the table, but instead of drinking it there, she took the mug and returned to the living room where she curled up in the corner of the sofa. After a tentative sip, she nodded. "This is good."

As she drank, she appraised him in that serious way she had. "How old were you when she left?"

For a moment, he could only stare at her in surprise. "What do you mean?"

She shrugged. "I just assumed your mom left, because you said your dad raised you alone. Also, when you talked about how your parents met, you said she never forgave your father for being just a man, which implies their marriage ended badly. Just now you said she made this for you when you were little. So I assume she left when you were pretty young. It sounds like it was a pretty nasty breakup."

"What makes you say that?" He avoided her gaze, even though there wasn't a hint of condemnation in her voice.

"I've sat on the bench for more than four years now. You get used to reading the signs."

"The signs?"

"The signs of a marriage gone wrong. Of husbands and wives fed up with each other. Of children disappointed by their parents' behavior. Disappointed by life. After a while you can hear it in the tone of their voice. See it in their expression. They seem haunted."

She sounded so sad as she spoke. And beneath that sorrow was the faintest hint of pity.

He leaned forward, bracing his elbows on his knees

and templing his fingers as he met her gaze. "I'm not a child. Don't make the mistake of treating me like one."

She blinked as if surprised by the ferocity of his tone. But she didn't back down, and her gaze didn't waver from his. "I didn't say you were. But we never get over the disappointments we suffer as a child, do we? Not the big ones, at least. Those disappointments can feel like abandonment—say, if mother doesn't stick around when things get tough."

Just like that, she'd summed up his entire childhood in one easy convenient package. And frankly, it ticked him off.

He stood and paced to the fireplace. "Don't try to psychoanalyze me."

"I wasn't trying to. I was just—"

"I don't feel abandoned by my mother. She did what she had to do."

"Deserting her husband and child? That was what she *had* to do?"

Kate sounded so damn logical. So reasonable. So irritating.

"Dad made her miserable. I can't say I blame her. She married a man she thought was a hero. Turned out he wasn't."

"You mentioned he was injured on the job. Was that when she left?"

"Neither of them really got over his injury. Dad started drinking. He had bouts of depression."

"So she didn't just leave you. She left you with an incompetent parent. That's borderline criminal."

"She did what she had to do."

"I'm sure she did," she muttered in a voice heavy with sarcasm.

He spun around to face her. His tone came out harsher than he'd intended. "Let it go, Kate. My family's not on trial here."

Kate flinched at his words, instantly stirring his guilt. She tried to hide her emotions, downing the last of the milk, but he saw the flash of pain in her eyes.

"Well, I'm sure you're right. I don't know what I'm talking about." She stood, taking her mug with her. "Thank you for the milk. I'm feeling sleepy already."

"Kate, I didn't mean…"

In the doorway to the hall, she looked over her shoulder. "Good night, Jake."

And then she disappeared, leaving him standing in the living room, alone. Again.

Eight

She had lied to him. She was not sleepy. The milk did not help. And she lay awake for what felt like several more hours, staring out the window, trying to figure out where things had gone wrong.

As far as she could tell, their conversation had been going along quite nicely…until she stuck her big fat nose where it didn't belong.

"Sounds like you had a troubled childhood, Jake," she murmured to herself in a whiny voice. "Why don't you tell me all about it while I poke you with a sharp stick."

With a huff, she rolled onto her other side. Who did she think she was? His therapist?

She sighed, running her hand over the curve of her belly. She hadn't meant to be nosy. Hadn't meant to venture where she wasn't wanted.

She'd just thought to…to what? Offer absolution of some kind?

Guilt came along with resenting a parent. That parent could be the worst person in the world—irresponsible, immoral or abusive—and yet nothing could overcome a child's basic need to love his parents. And if that love eventually soured and faded, the child inevitably felt a certain amount of guilt.

She'd wrestled with those emotions herself for years before finally admitting that it was okay to be angry with her birth mother for abandoning them to the imperfect mercies of the Texas foster care system and with her adopted mom for loving Beth so much. Doing so had helped her finally make peace with her adopted mom. Though she'd never be as close to her as Beth was, at least they now talked occasionally. So often she saw those conflicting emotions on the faces of the children whose warring parents paraded them through her court.

Of course, making peace with her own emotions and pushing Jake to acknowledge his were two very different things. Perhaps it was for the best that he'd pushed back. After all, she was supposed to be maintaining her distance from him, not forging an emotional connection.

She thought of the baby growing within her. She was already so much more attached to this baby than she should be. Even though she had no intention of keeping the baby, part of her still yearned…for what? Some fairy tale ending in which she and Jake fell in love, decided to keep the baby and lived happily ever after?

The very thought was absurd. She'd learned long ago that happily ever afters weren't for her. The lesson she was taught by an uncaring mother and an impersonal social services system had only been reinforced by the men she'd dated. Men who'd found her independence annoying and her strong will troublesome. Jake would most likely be no different.

No, she'd learned long ago it was best to stand on her own two feet. To depend only on herself rather than on others. That was the only way to keep from getting hurt.

Yes, keeping her distance from Jake was crucial. Because the unseen bonds between them were already far too strong.

By the time morning rolled around, Kate was exhausted. Days of too little sleep, combined with nerves and the pregnancy, had worn her down. Still, she found herself unable to doze any longer. So she got out of bed around six, dressed, and headed for breakfast.

She stopped cold in the doorway. Jake sat at the kitchen table, the morning paper open in front of him, a mug of coffee cradled in one hand, a last bite of a croissant sitting on a plate.

Unsure if she was up for another confrontation, she eased back a step, hoping to sneak away unnoticed. But he raised his head and pinned her with his stare.

"You're up early."

Overcome by the sudden need to fidget, she had to make herself stand perfectly still. "So are you." She'd been sure that after his late night he'd still be in bed. Yet once again he surprised her.

"I figured you'd be up early. Since you've been having trouble sleeping." He motioned to the white paper bag in the center of the table. "I got you a whole wheat banana nut muffin. Giselle at the bakery said that's what you normally get."

The unexpected gesture warmed her. Last night she'd trampled all over his personal space—emotionally speaking—and yet this morning he'd still been thoughtful enough to get her breakfast.

Despite her promises to herself not to rely on him,

she couldn't bring herself to reject his peace offering. So she pulled out the chair across from his and tugged the bag toward her.

She tore the bag down the side and spread the paper out before her as a makeshift plate. To her surprise, she found not just the whole wheat banana nut muffin, but a chocolate raspberry croissant, as well.

Before she could protest, he jumped up to get her a glass of milk. "I didn't know what you were in the mood for," he said as he also handed her a plate.

As she stared at the choices before her, her self-control wavered. The whole wheat banana nut muffin was indisputably the right choice. The healthy choice. Better for her, better for the baby.

But she yearned for the chocolate raspberry croissant…as completely devoid of nutritional value and as laden with calories and fat as it was. Just looking at it made her taste buds prickle and her stomach growl.

She felt as if every emotional battle she'd waged in her life came down to this. What she knew was best versus what she desperately wanted.

In the end she knew she'd do what she always did. The right thing. Because if she didn't make the right choice, she certainly couldn't trust anyone else to do so, either. And this time, more than her own wants and needs were at stake. She was making this choice for the baby, as well.

With one last look at the croissant, she put the muffin on her plate and carefully wrapped the paper bag around the croissant.

She peeled back the paper on the muffin and tore off a bite. As she popped it in her mouth, she noticed Jake smiling.

"What?"

He shook his head wryly. "Somehow I knew you'd pick the muffin."

"There's caffeine in chocolate."

"Not much more than there is in your decaf coffee," he pointed out.

"The muffin is still the better choice. Whole wheat, protein from the nuts and even a little fruit. Lots of nutrients the baby needs."

"Sure." He nodded.

"You disagree?"

"Not at all. That's very logical. You're taking this surrogate mother thing very seriously."

"Of course I am," she admitted. "This is a huge responsibility."

"And you feel like you have to do everything just perfect."

"You say that like it's a bad thing." And then, because she didn't want to sound defensive, she added lightly, "Besides, I'm the only one who can."

"Well, sure, but…"

"But…" she prodded.

He held up the last bite of his own croissant. "But sometimes you have to spoil yourself. Just a little."

As she watched, he placed that last bite in his mouth. She could just imagine how it tasted. The sweet chocolate, the lingering tartness of the raspberries. The way the flakes of croissant would practically melt on her tongue.

By comparison, her muffin tasted dry and bland. No contrast. No depth. No decadence.

An unexpected wave of sadness hit her. Usually she liked banana nut muffins. She'd eaten them for breakfast without complaint for years.

Now she wondered if she'd ever enjoy one again.

Resolutely, she took another bite of the muffin and

forced herself to chew and swallow. After washing down the bite with a gulp of milk, she said, "I wanted to—"

"About last night—"

Laughing, Jake ducked his head, looking up at her from beneath his lashes. "You go first."

Kate felt the power of that glance deep in her belly. There was a rueful, almost bashful, gleam in his eyes that was way more appealing than his usually wicked charm. Which was saying a lot, since she often found his usually wicked charm pretty dang hard to resist.

Determined not to make a fool of herself if she could avoid it, she sucked in a deep breath and dove head-first into her groveling. "I wanted to apologize for last night. I didn't mean to pry into matters none of my business."

There was more she wanted to say, so she stuffed a chunk of muffin in her mouth to quiet herself.

"It's funny." He took a sip of his coffee. "I was going to apologize for being so defensive. I guess I'm just not used to talking about her."

"Well, most people have decent relationships with their moms. And if you do, it's hard to imagine a mom who's a little more difficult to get along with."

"Actually, we have a pretty good relationship now."

Her eyebrows shot up and she eyed him with doubt. "You have to have some lingering anger toward your mother."

"I don't." He shrugged with a nonchalance she didn't buy. "I did when I was young, but we get along fine now."

"So your mother abandoned you and you've just… what? Just forgiven her?"

"Yes. Why is that so hard for you to believe?"

She pushed back her chair, snatched up the remains of her breakfast and took them to them trash can. "It just is, okay?" She stomped on the foot lever that popped the top to the can and dumped her trash inside.

As the lid clanged closed, she realized how snappish she sounded. What a way to apologize.

She turned back to face him and leaned against the counter behind her. "I only meant that if you do have any lingering resentment, it'd be best to admit it. Parents are imperfect, too. It's okay to be angry with them."

He leveled his gaze at her. "Kate, it's also okay to forgive them."

Ah, so they weren't talking about just his mother anymore.

"What's that supposed to mean?" she asked, even though she suspected she knew exactly what he meant. His appraisal was too intense for her to miss his implication.

"You've never even tried to make peace with your mother, have you?"

"Make peace with her? No. Sorry. I can't make peace with what she did."

"Still—"

"The state took us away when Beth was ten and I was eight. Mom didn't even protest. Never tried to get us back." A sarcastic laugh struggled past her lips. "Maybe you think I should be grateful. Maybe letting us go was the best thing she ever did for us."

Jake just eyed her with what she was sure was pity. "All these years later and you're still letting the way she treated you affect your life."

"And I suppose now you're going to point out that Beth has handled this whole thing so much better than I have. That she—miraculously—has overcome all the hardships of our childhood, made peace with our mother's actions and learned to trust again."

"No," he said quietly. "I wasn't going to say any of that. This isn't about Beth. It's about you."

Suddenly her exhaustion caught up with her and she slumped against the counter. God, she hated it when she felt like this. Angry and bitter. Not just at her mother, but at everyone involved in her upbringing. All the overworked caseworkers who didn't have the time to do their jobs properly. All the foster parents who'd judged and found her lacking.

Sometimes—she was most ashamed to admit—she was even angry with Beth, who'd seemed to have such an easier time being shuttled from foster house to foster house. Who'd instantly been everyone's favorite and who seemed never to feel unwanted.

She forced herself to hold his gaze. "I guess you're right. It's not about Beth. But…"

"But…" he prodded.

"But sometimes I wish I was more like her. She coped with things differently than I did. Plus, our experiences have been different. She and Stew met and fell in love so young. For most of her life, she's had him to depend on. To trust. I've never had that." Uncomfortable with the personal turn of the conversation, she looked away.

God, she didn't want him to think she was fishing for something from him, so she forced an upbeat tone into her voice. "I've always been very self-reliant. That's the way I like it. I'm the one person I know I can always trust."

The smile she gave him felt tight. His gaze seemed to pierce right through her forced cheer, and she had to turn away from him to hide.

Rinsing her breakfast dishes proved the perfect diversion. But when she was done, she turned to find Jake standing right behind her.

Before she could protest, he pulled her gently to his

chest. Stroking her hair, he murmured. "There's nothing wrong with the way you've coped with things. You're strong and brave. And that's admirable. But you're not alone anymore. I'm here to help. You can trust me."

His arms felt so good around her. So strong and capable. His chest was solid beneath her cheek. His shoulders broad. Her eyes drifted closed, and she allowed herself to lean against him. He seemed so solid. So dependable. So much what she'd always wanted and never allowed herself.

Oh, how she wanted to believe him. To pretend, just for a few minutes, that he could share her burdens. That his presence in her life wasn't temporary.

He meant well, but in the end he was like that chocolate raspberry croissant. A temptation she didn't dare allow herself to enjoy.

Nine

By the time Kate arrived home Friday evening, Jake had already left for work and wouldn't return until after midnight. Normally he worked the day shift four days a week, but tonight he was covering for a buddy on vacation.

She wandered restlessly through the house, amazed that she'd become accustomed to his presence. Even though they rarely spent time together, she'd gotten used to having him around.

What would it be like once this was all over with and he left for good? She'd have neither him nor the baby to keep her company. The thought made her inexplicably sad.

No matter how many times she reminded herself that neither Jake nor the baby were hers to keep, she couldn't help wishing... *Wishing what?* the more logical part of her mind scoffed.

Keeping the baby was out of the question, no matter what she secretly yearned for. As for keeping Jake, what would be the point? She'd been independent her entire adult life. She relied on no one but herself for her happiness, and that was the way she wanted it. It was the only way to ensure she'd never be let down, never be hurt. She'd had more than enough of that during her childhood.

Still, she couldn't help wondering what it would be like if they were a different sort of newlywed couple.

Undoubtedly, she'd wait up for him. Plan some romantic encounter for when he got home after work. Pull out the lingerie she'd bought before the wedding and spend the evening relaxing in a tub scented with exotic oils. Or maybe she'd retire early after planning a romantic breakfast in bed for him the next morning.

Kate felt a slight throbbing deep in her gut in response to the images her mind had conjured. She would do none of those things, and the evening stretched endlessly before her.

Around eight, she opened the fridge, planning to make herself a grilled cheese sandwich, only to find a casserole dish with a note from Jake taped to the lid.

Don't worry, it's good for you. Lasagna with lots of veggies and whole wheat pasta. Maybe you'll eat the chocolate croissant for dessert.

She smiled. Like this morning, she couldn't bring herself to reject his peace offering. Besides, what he'd prepared was much better for the baby than the grilled cheese she would have made. So she nuked the lasagna in the microwave and ate it at the kitchen table with a glass of milk while reviewing papers. By the time her plate was clean and the last of her work seen to, fatigue settled over her like a heavy blanket.

She tried to nap on the sofa, but couldn't get comfortable. Her own bed was worse, inexplicably both lumpy and hard. Then she remembered what Jake had said about his mattress.

It helped him sleep like the dead.

She grabbed the pillows from her bed and marched down the hall to his room.

She stood in the doorway for a long moment just staring at his bed. She hadn't been in this room since he moved in, and somehow the changes surprised her.

His king-size bed was huge. He hadn't made the bed that morning, so the thick navy comforter remained pulled back, revealing cream-colored sheets beneath. A heavy dresser lined one wall and a chair sat in a corner, both draped in discarded clothes. The room looked…comfortably messy. Lived in. This was most definitely *his* space. And *she* was invading it.

She'd never dream of doing something like this, if she didn't need some decent sleep so desperately.

Just a few hours of decent sleep and she'd sneak back to her own bed.

Jake wouldn't be home for hours. He'd never know. After all, with her recent sleep patterns, she'd be awake long before he got home, to sneak back to her own bed.

She slid between his sheets. They were soft, worn from years of use, and they felt good against the skin of her arms and legs, left bare by the tap pants and camisole she wore—the last of her prepregnancy pajamas that still fit.

After propping her own pillows against her back, she curled into a ball on her left side and burrowed her face into his pillow. With every breath, she inhaled the scent of him, crisp and clean, with a slight hint of masculine muskiness.

And for the first time in weeks—maybe months—she relaxed into sleep.

* * *

When Jake pulled into the driveway a little past midnight, not a single light shone through the windows.

Inside, the house was quiet and Kate's bedroom door was closed. He could only hope she was finally getting some sleep.

Not wanting to wake her, he crept into the kitchen to make himself a sandwich. To his delight, he saw that Kate had eaten the lasagna he made for her dinner. But not the croissant. Well, at least he was making some progress.

He took a quick shower to rinse off the grime from sifting through the remains of the fire, and planned to read a little of his Dean Koontz book in bed before calling it a night.

Only, when he walked into his bedroom, a bath towel wrapped around his waist, he found a Kate-size lump in the center of his bed and realized reading wasn't going to be an option.

"Looks like someone's been sleeping in my bed," he murmured.

He crept closer, to get a better look. She was curled into a ball on her side, her fist tucked under her chin, like an infant. Her inky hair spilled across his pillow. Her bare shoulder and the thin strap of something silky and decadent, were visible above the sheets.

His resolve to keep his distance seemed suddenly doomed.

She was his wife.

She was carrying his baby.

And she was asleep in his bed.

The same bed he'd lain awake in countless nights thinking about her. Trying to piece together the puzzle of Kate. And—if he was honest with himself—wanting her.

And all she wanted was a good night's sleep.

He couldn't give her even half the things he wanted to, but he could give her that, at least.

As quietly as he could, he pulled a pair of boxers and sweat shorts from the dresser drawer. With his back to her, he yanked them on. He was creeping to the door when she made a cute little sniffling noise in her sleep, followed by a soft moan. He spun to look at her, waiting to see if she'd woken.

She wasn't fully awake, but as soon as she started to roll onto her back, her eyes flew open. When she spotted him standing at the foot of the bed, she sat bolt upright, clutching the sheet to her chest.

"I…I…"

He held his hands palms out to calm her. "It's okay."

"No, it's not." She swung her legs over the side of the bed, but she must have still been groggy and lightheaded, because she never made it to standing. "I didn't… I'm so embarrassed." She propped her elbows on her knees and buried her face in her hands. "I thought you wouldn't be home for hours."

She looked so adorably flustered, he couldn't resist comforting her. So against his better judgment, he rounded the bed to sit by her side.

"Hey, it's okay."

She peered at him through the cracks in her fingers. "What time is it?"

He glanced at the clock beside his bed, which apparently she hadn't seen. "A little after one."

She curled her fingers in so her chin was propped in her palms. "I slept for four hours. How is it possible I'm still tired?"

Her hair hung mussed about her face, with one heavy lock draped in front of her eyes. Almost of their own volition, his fingers rose to brush aside that lock of hair. "It's been how many days since you had a decent night's sleep?"

She scrubbed a hand across her face and sat up straighter. "Quite a few. Weeks, maybe." She stood, swaying slightly on her feet. "I guess I'll head back to my own bed."

For some reason he just couldn't pin down, he didn't want to let her do that. He grabbed her wrist. "Wait."

Her skin was warm and he could have sworn he felt her pulse leap under his fingers. You should stay here," he said.

Her eyes widened and she pulled her wrist from his hand. Her gaze darted to his bare chest, and he would have sworn he saw a flash of awareness in her eyes.

Tempting as hell, but not exactly what he'd had in mind.

He leaped to his feet before he said or did something really stupid. "Look, obviously you slept better in here than you have in your own bed. It only makes sense for you to sleep the rest of the night in here. It's just for tonight. You'll feel better in the morning."

He took her hand again and tugged her gently toward the bed. To his surprise she let him. The second she sat down on the bed, she seemed to relax.

"Where will you sleep?"

"I'll figure something out," he reassured her as he nudged her shoulder back.

She lay down, curling onto her side so that her back faced him.

"I won't be able to sleep," she muttered, her eyes already closed, the lines of fatigue on her face easing.

"Just give it a few minutes." He had the strongest urge to brush her hair back from her face, but leaned over her and murmured. "If you don't fall back asleep, you can get up and I'll take you dancing."

She chuckled, then sighed as she began to nod off. For a long moment he stood there, watching her. There was something so peaceful about watching someone sleep. So intimate. In that moment, he was seeing a side of her few people ever saw.

With a sigh of his own, he crept to the chair in the corner to retrieve one of the shirts draped across its back. He was reaching for the novel on his bedside table, when she started to roll over onto her back and once again jerked awake.

She blinked sleepily. "See, I told you I wouldn't fall asleep."

He sat down on the side of the bed and gave in to the urge to run his hand down her hair. "You were asleep. You just woke up when you nearly rolled over."

She groaned and buried her face against the pillow. "It's silly that I'm so worried about sleeping wrong, isn't it?"

"No."

She looked over her shoulder at him. "How long was I asleep this time?"

"Not long enough."

Then inspiration hit. He climbed into bed beside her and pulled her back against his chest so his body cradled hers.

"Jake!" she protested, trying to pull away from him.

"Shhh…it's okay," he murmured. "I'm just trying to help. You can't sleep because you're afraid of rolling over, right? Well, if I'm here, you won't roll over."

"But—"

"If you know you can't roll over, you'll be able to sleep."

She let out a puff of air. "Theoretically. But—"

"You can trust me." He chuckled to ease her fears,

even though there was nothing funny about having her body pressed against his. "I promise I won't take advantage of you."

"That's not what I'm worried about. No one would want to take advantage of a woman who's almost five months pregnant." She twisted to look at him over her shoulder. "But this is exactly the kind of intimacy we agreed it best we didn't share."

"I won't tell if you don't."

Again he smoothed her hair down with his palm and then, because he didn't know what to do with his hand, he rested it on her shoulder. She began to relax against him incrementally.

Just when he thought she'd fallen asleep, she said, "I'm just worried about doing everything right."

"I know you are." She tried so hard to make all the right choices for the baby. How could he help but admire that?

"I want…the baby…to be healthy and strong." She sounded as if she were struggling to stay awake. "I don't want…to disappoint Beth and Stew…. Or you."

He sucked in a breath, waiting to see if she'd say anything to explain that cryptic comment. But apparently she'd fallen asleep because she said nothing else.

Staring down at her, he couldn't help but be a little amazed. Until this moment he'd had no idea she was afraid of doing everything right. But wasn't that just like her? To keep her fears and concerns to herself?

He urged his body to relax, but found it impossible to do so. With her lavender-scented hair tickling his nose, her lush fertile body resting against his, and her warm round bottom nestled against his groin, it was all he could do to continue breathing regularly.

It was going to be a long night.

* * *

Kate woke feeling rested for the first time in weeks. Not just rested…secure. Safe. Completely at peace.

Slowly she became aware of her surroundings.

And of Jake nestled against her back.

The events of the previous night came rushing back. The embarrassment of being found sleeping in his bed, which just barely exceeded her embarrassment at being talked into staying there.

Oh, boy. This had not gone as planned.

The worst part was, she didn't immediately leap from the bed and preserve whatever dignity she had left. Lying next to Jake just felt too dang good.

With his chest cradling her back, his hand resting on her belly and the warm masculine scent of him surrounding her, whatever willpower she had possessed deserted her completely.

His breath, slow and even across her ear, sent tremors of pleasure radiating through her body and she just couldn't resist nestling deeper under the covers, closer to him.

Only then did she realize that the lean muscles of his chest and arms weren't the only parts of his body that were hard and unyielding. She felt a jolt of pure anticipation.

How long had it been since she'd woken up in a man's bed? Suddenly, it seemed like years. Geesh, maybe it was years. Long enough that she'd forgotten the intimacy that came from sleeping with another person.

Saturday-morning sex had always been her favorite. Slow and lazy. Relaxed almost. With no rush, no constraints on time. Just the steady building of passion and the ecstasy of release.

Before she could give in to temptation, she started

to pull away, but stilled when Jake's arm tightened over her belly.

"Don't go," he murmured against her ear.

She sucked in a breath. "You're awake?"

"Barely."

He sounded sleepy, but not just-woke-up sleepy. She twisted her head just enough to shoot him a suspicious look. "How long have you been awake?"

Propping himself up on an elbow, he looked down at her without removing his hand from her belly. "Long enough to feel you wake up."

He'd lain there beside her. His erection pressing against her buttocks, but saying nothing. Not even moving. Her pulse kicked up a notch. Was he as aroused as she was? Or was this just a standard physical response for him?

"And you didn't move?"

"I didn't want to wake you."

His answer was so simple. So logical.

Still, having him so close made her feel as if she could crawl out of her skin. "You should have—"

Just then the baby gave her a sharp jab, right under Jake's hand.

"Oh my God. Was that…?"

She again started to pull away from him. "I should really—"

He didn't let her get very far, but lassoed her with an arm and pulled her back to his side. Before she knew what was happening, he had her flat on her back and was pressing the side of his face as well as his hand to her stomach.

"You know—" she tried to protest.

"Shh," he said.

"It's not like you'll be able to hear her."

"Shh."

"I'm not supposed to be on my back like this."

"It's only for a minute," he said without moving his head.

Well, at least he wasn't shushing her anymore.

As much as she hated to admit it, he was probably right. A few minutes on her back couldn't do much harm. Which was kind of a shame, because she really could have used the excuse to get out from under him.

With his face pressed to her belly, she could feel the warmth of his breath through her camisole. And when she inhaled, she could feel the prickle of his unshaved cheek poking through the silky thin fabric.

His hand pressed low across her abdomen, his palm hot against her. Especially where the camisole didn't quite meet the top of her tap pants and he touched bare skin. If he lowered his hand just a few inches—five, maybe six, at most—he'd be touching her intimately. And her traitorous body wished desperately that he would.

It would be so easy to rock her hips up to his touch.

She sucked in a deep breath and squeezed her eyes closed. Boy, she hoped he couldn't hear the thundering of her heart. But how could he not? He wasn't deaf. Hoping to cover the sound, she said, "Jake, I really don't think this is—"

The baby gave another sharp kick, right to the spot where his cheek rested.

This time, they both sucked in deep breaths.

"I felt that." Awe laced his words. "I definitely felt that." Without moving his left hand from her belly, he raised up on his other elbow and looked at her. His goofy expression nearly took her breath away again. "Damn, that's something."

She could only nod in response.

"Was this the first time you felt her move?"

"No."

His smile faded. "And you didn't say anything?"

"I—" She bit down on her lip.

"How long have you felt her moving?"

"Three weeks. Maybe four. It's hard to say." His expression urged her to try, so she fumbled to explain. "At first it was so vague. I wasn't sure that's what I was even feeling. The doctor said it would feel like a fluttering. Like butterfly wings. But that's not what it felt like at all."

"What was it like? I mean, what is it like?"

He was staring at her so intently her throat nearly closed up on her. No one had ever looked at her so closely. Watched her with such an expression of curiosity. As if her next words would be the most important he'd ever hear.

"It's more like—" she struggled to put the sensation into words "—a twitch. Like a muscle spasm. Or maybe…" Then she hit on the perfect description. "Do you know the feeling when you're really nervous or you've been exercising really hard and you can feel your heart thundering in your chest?"

He nodded without taking his eyes from her face. His voice, when he spoke, was husky with emotion. "Yeah. I know what you mean."

For an instant her mind went completely blank and she lost herself in his gaze. Her entire existence seemed to shrink down to just him. Just this moment. Just his hand on her stomach, the look in his eyes, and the thundering of her heart.

Right…her thundering heart. The movement of the baby. That was what they'd been talking about.

She forced herself to finish her description, but her voice sounded breathless and weak. "That's what it's like. Like your heart beating against your ribs. But not rhythmic."

He looked back at her belly when the baby once again moved against his hand. "It's amazing."

"Yes." She nearly choked on the words. "It is amazing."

It truly was amazing. Not just the sensation of her baby moving inside her, but the way he'd looked at her.

No one had ever looked at her like that before. As if *she* was amazing. And she'd never in her whole life felt closer to another person.

She felt part of something far bigger and more important than any of the other things in her life—duty, justice, honor. Things she'd always thought of as so hugely important, but that seemed dwarfed by this baby and the connection it created between her and Jake.

It nearly broke her heart to think that this was all just an illusion. The connection she felt was not just frail; it was false.

Because the baby wasn't hers. And neither was Jake.

Ten

Kate had been distant from the moment she climbed out of his bed Saturday morning. She went out for breakfast and spent the day in her office. His only consolation was that she'd agreed to go to a barbecue with him on Sunday at a buddy's house. That would give him the whole day with her. A whole day full of excuses to hold and touch her.

When she finally did make it back to the house that night, she refused to sleep in his bed again. Even when he offered to take the sofa…which he thought was more than generous.

After several hours of staring at the ceiling, missing having Kate in his bed after only one night, Jake was finally almost asleep when he heard a low moan coming from Kate's room.

In an instant all his senses went to high alert and he was out of his bed and running down the hall.

Her door was shut. Without thinking, he twisted the knob at the same time he slammed his shoulder against the door. It flew open and ricocheted against the wall. He didn't bother searching for the bedroom light. There was no need. Light shone in through the window, revealing a tableau of Kate sitting up in bed bent over her leg. When he'd crashed through the door, she turned toward the noise, and now her face was clearly illuminated in the moonlight.

"What's wrong?" he asked frantically.

"Just a leg cramp," she said, turning her attention back to her leg.

Relief flashed through him. She wasn't sick. The baby was fine. Nothing was wrong.

Except that she was in pain. The thought pulled him to her side.

"Let me help." He lowered himself to the edge of her bed.

"I've got it," she muttered, trying to wiggle away from him. But her movements must have made the cramp worse, because she winced noticeably and reached again for her leg.

He blocked her hands with his palm. "Let me help."

She eyed him warily in the near dark but finally relented, leaning back onto her elbows, granting him free access to her leg.

He'd had leg cramps before and knew they could be painful, so he moved slowly. Taking the heel of her foot in one hand, he ran his other down the length of her calf. He gently massaged the tense muscles, willing himself to focus on the task, rather than the length of bare leg exposed to him.

He could go on forever touching her skin…sitting in her bed. If he thought for even a minute that she'd let him.

As much as he wanted to lose himself in the pleasure

of touching her, he tried to restrain his reaction. He was a certified EMT. He should have been able to detach himself from the situation. But he couldn't. Not with her. Not when he'd spent all day wanting her. Resisting her. Not when he'd spent all day wanting her. He just wasn't that strong. No man was.

His thumb found a particularly hard knot. As he tried to loosen it, she groaned. The sound was low and guttural and threatened his willpower.

But it also brought him back to his senses. She was in pain, not turned on.

He looked up at her face, trying to read her expression, but her eyes were closed, her head tilted back, exposing the length of her arched neck. "Too hard?"

Her head came up and her eyes blinked open. "No. It feels good."

"I'm going to try to stretch the muscle, okay?"

She nodded, her eyes wide.

Watching her carefully for signs of pain, he grasped the ball of her foot and slowly flexed. Her expression didn't even flicker. If she was in pain, she wasn't showing it.

He couldn't help but admire how tough she was. So independent, so sure of herself, so determined. Qualities he never thought about wanting in a wife. But he was glad she had them.

He flexed her foot several more times until he felt the knot beneath his thumb loosen and dissolve.

"Better?"

She nodded. "I'm sorry I woke you."

"Don't apologize. And don't pretend this isn't much harder on you than it is on me."

Even though the cramping had stopped, he couldn't seem to make himself release her leg. The soft spot just behind her knee was too tempting. He kept expecting her to pull her leg away from his touch, but she didn't.

Her lips curved into a half smile. "Well, maybe a little harder."

He shifted his weight, moving closer to her on the bed. As he did, his hand slipped from her calf to just above her knee. With his free hand, he brushed aside the lock of hair that had fallen into her eyes.

There were a thousand things he wanted to tell her. How beautiful she looked in the moonlight. How tempting her skin felt. How enticing she smelled. How much he wanted to kiss her.

How he'd wanted to kiss her all day.

Before he let any of those things slip, he forced himself to remember his past mistakes. Even the slightest nudge, and she'd scamper in the other direction.

So he shoved aside all the things he wanted to say and instead said the one thing he didn't think would spook her. "Has the baby been moving?"

"She's been a little active today. But I feel her more at night."

"You keep referring to the baby as a 'her.' Has the doctor—"

"No. It's just a gut feeling."

They were so close. In the half light from the moon, he saw her eyes widen. He heard her soft intake of breath. He wanted desperately to kiss her but knew he couldn't. She'd set out strict ground rules for their marriage.

For the first time in his life, alone with a beautiful woman in her bedroom he found himself wishing they were in a crowded place.

He forced himself to withdraw his hands and lean back. Now, if only he could force himself to return to his room. But, hey, he wasn't a saint.

Before he could chastise himself any more, she surprised him by asking, "What were you thinking just now?"

He surprised himself even more by answering. "I was wishing we were in public. If we were, I'd have an excuse to kiss you."

She leaned forward, her gaze dropping to his mouth. "You've never seemed like the kind of man who needs an excuse to do what he wants."

Hell, he had a hundred reasons to break the rules. And only one reason not to. If he did, he'd lose her. That was the one thing he wasn't willing to risk.

Still, there was a hint of invitation in her eyes. But how could he take advantage of her? How could he destroy the trust they'd only just started to build?

He stood, putting some distance between them. "Don't tempt me, Kate."

She stiffened. "I don't know what you mean."

"Sure, you do. You made me promise this would be only a business arrangement. No intimacy. Those were your rules."

Defiance flashed in her eyes as she met his gaze. "So?"

"If you want to change the rules, then *you* have to change them. I won't break them for you."

But, damn, he wanted to.

So much so that he continued to stand there, watching her, when he knew he should leave. Before he went back on his word and did exactly what he'd sworn he wouldn't do.

She swung her legs over the side of the bed and stood. "What if I want to change the rules?"

His heart started pounding in his chest. Urging him to kiss her. To make her his.

It'd be so easy to give in to his heart. But impossible to justify to his conscience.

Unless he was sure this was what she really wanted.

"They're your rules. You're the only one who can change them."

He was right, of course. They were her rules. She was the one who'd insisted there be no intimacy between them. He was just following the guidelines she'd set out for them. And, frankly, it was annoying the hell out of her.

Was it too much to ask—really?—that he just sweep her into his arms and kiss her senseless? Would that really be so hard on him?

For once in her life, she didn't want to think. Didn't want to be the responsible one. Didn't want to have to make a decision.

She knew he desired her. Felt it in his touch and every look. But she wanted more than just desire. She wanted complete and total surrender. She wanted him to be unable to resist her.

There were a hundred ways they were wrong for each other. She wanted them to be right for each other in this one way.

Slowly she stood before him, close enough that she could see his eyes dilate, even in the dim lighting. Close enough to see the individual hairs scattered across his bare chest. Close enough to smell the warm, masculine scent of him. The same scent that had permeated his pillow the night before.

Was it so wrong to want this?

It didn't feel wrong. In fact, nothing had ever felt more right. What could be more right than making love with the father of her child? What could be more natural?

That thought drummed through her mind as she worked up the courage to raise her hand to his cheek. She could feel the pulse at his temple thundering beneath her fingertips. His heart seemed to beat in the

same crazy rhythm as her own. One thump for anticipation, one for fear. One for pure desire.

As her hand slipped down to cup his jaw, she reveled
in the coarse prickle of hair against her palm. Hoping
to tempt him into submission, she stood on tiptoe and
raised her lips to his.

But he stubbornly pulled away. "Don't do this, Kate."

"Don't do what?" Unable to reach his lips, she
pressed her mouth to his jaw. "Don't do this?"

His skin was hot. The stubble of his beard rough
against her lips. She couldn't resist trailing her lips
down the enticing column of his throat. "Or don't do
this?"

There was something heady about the faint saltiness of
his skin. About the feel of his pulse thundering beneath
her lips. Feeling off balance and a little dizzy, she plastered her palms to his naked chest, thrilling at the sensation of his muscles clenching beneath her touch. "Or this?"

He stared down at her with such intensity. Such restrained power.

Honestly, she couldn't have said what appealed to her
more. His sheer strength or the control he maintained
over it.

She only knew, in that instant, that his personality
was far stronger than she'd previously realized. His
laid-back, casual attitude had fooled herself into under-
estimating his strength of will.

That strength spoke to her in a way she never would
have predicted. She was drawn to his strength and power.
Wanting—somewhat desperately—to be *his* weakness.

"Why shouldn't we give in to what we both want?"
she asked.

He clamped his hands over hers, stopping their
progress. "Because it's the middle of the night. People

do stupid things at 3:00 a.m. They don't think right. They're not logical. They make mistakes."

His arguments were certainly reasonable. But she heard the faint tremor in his voice. The underlying roughness that told her she affected him more than he wanted to admit.

"You're right," she admitted, but pressed on before he could assume she was admitting defeat. "Sometimes people do stupid things in the middle of the night. But sometimes they do brave things. Bold things. Things they'd never have the courage to do in broad daylight."

Much to her chagrin, he chuckled. "Katie, you're the last woman I can imagine needing to bolster her courage."

"Just shows you how good I am at faking it." The admission seemed to lift a weight off her shoulders, so she continued, "I've spent too many months worried about making mistakes. But the one mistake I won't let myself make is being too stubborn to admit I was wrong.

"I know I said I wanted no intimacy between us. I know I insisted on that, but I was wrong. I didn't know how hard it would be to live with you. I never imagined how much I'd want you."

That admission seemed to do the trick. In an instant he went from hard and unyielding to completely at her mercy. She saw the acquiescence in his eyes. Felt it in his touch.

This time, when she stood on her toes to kiss him, he lowered his mouth to hers.

She marveled at the mastery of his kiss. How the simple act of pressing his mouth to hers made her blood pulse and desire quicken in her belly.

As soon as he released her hands, she wrapped her arms around his neck, eagerly pressing her body to his. Just a thin layer of fabric separated them, but it felt like too much. As if he read her mind, his hands moved to the hem of her nightshirt. For a second his fingers merely toyed with the edge, tempting her. Teasing her. But then his hand slipped beneath the hem to her hip. His fingers were rough against her already sensitized skin, eliciting a moan from deep within her.

She grew impatient with his gentle coaxing. She wanted his hands on her—all over her—now.

She grasped the hem of her shirt and pulled her mouth from his long enough to yank the offensive garment over her head.

He stepped back, and for an instant she feared he would leave. But his expression told her he had no intention of going anywhere. He merely studied her.

She felt a curious blossoming of pride. His gaze was heated with desire. His expression taut with barely restrained control. He wanted her and made no attempt to hide it.

"Oh, man, you're beautiful." His words were low and rough. And soft, almost as if he hadn't really meant to say them aloud.

He reached out a finger to trace the curve of her breast. She could have sworn there was a slight tremble in his hand as his finger moved down the slope of her breast to circle the nipple.

Her breasts were so tender that when he finally cupped her in his hands, she groaned aloud with a pleasure so intense it was almost painful.

Instantly his hands stilled. "Too much?"

She shook her head. His touch was far too gentle to cause pain. Far too cautious. "Perfect," she gasped. "Just perfect."

There were so many things she wanted to tell him. How she'd dreamed of this moment. Ached for it. How she'd lain awake in her bed, not just because she couldn't sleep, but because she wanted him there with her. Touching her just like this.

He sat on the edge of the bed and pulled her toward him to stand between his legs. At first he merely nuzzled her breasts, licking lightly at her nipples. Testing her endurance. Unable to take any more of his teasing, she ran her fingers through his hair and urged his mouth to her.

As if he read her mind, he clamped his lips down on her nipple, sucking it fully into his mouth. Pleasure spiked through her so intense her knees nearly gave out. Clutching his shoulders, she leaned into him to keep her balance. Soon, even this intense pleasure wasn't enough for her. She wanted—no needed—to feel him inside of her. Needed him to ease the ache that pulsed between her legs.

But she wouldn't beg.

So instead, she took control.

Pushing against his shoulders, she urged him back onto the bed. After slipping out of her panties, she climbed on his lap.

For a moment she had to close her eyes against the pleasure of it. His erection straining against his pajama bottoms pressed into the folds of skin between her legs. The sensation brought momentary relief to her aching flesh. But it lasted only a heartbeat before her desperation redoubled.

She brought her mouth down to his. Into that kiss she poured all the need she wouldn't allow herself to voice. She didn't just want him. She wanted to drive him crazy. She wanted him as out of control as she felt. No, more out of control.

She moved her hands across his chest, reveling in the tensing of hard muscles and the pounding of his heart. But she didn't linger there. Instead she sought the waistband of his pants. Sensing her intention, he raised his hips off the bed long enough to slip the pants down to his thighs.

She didn't give him a chance to do more than that, but immediately sank down to press against his bare skin.

His erection was hot, like the insistent pulsing between her legs. She didn't even try to resist the urge to rub herself against his length, arching her back and neck as she lost herself in the moment of pleasure.

Jake grabbed her hips, stilling her movement. "Wait," he gasped. His voice was deep, his expression taut with desire.

"Too much?" she asked.

"Perfect. Just perfect," he said, echoing her words. "But too perfect. I want to be inside you." He started to roll out from under her. "I think I have a box of condoms somewhere in my—"

Planting her hands firmly on his shoulders, she held him in place. "No need. I'm already pregnant and we were both tested for everything before—" An uneasy stab of something like jealousy hit her square in the chest. "Unless, since then you've—"

"No. I haven't been with anyone else since then."

She knew he hadn't been with anyone since they married, but four months had passed from when he had donated to when they had married. Anything could have happened in those four months.

She leaned over him, mere inches from his face, looking directly into his eyes. His gaze held not even a flicker of deception.

She wanted to believe him. Her gut and intuition—not to mention her years of experience looking into people's eyes to ascertain if they were lying—told her she could trust him.

But a lifetime of being cautious kept her from taking that leap.

She rolled off him to dig through the drawer of her nightstand and pull out a condom. As she tore it open, she met his gaze. Only the slightest hint of an emotion flickered through his eyes, but it was gone before she could even begin to guess how he felt. Holding up the condom, she asked, "Have I ruined the mood?"

Holding her breath, she waited for his answer. And for a second she thought he might not respond. But then he sat up.

Wrapping one arm around her waist, he pulled her to him and brought his mouth to hers.

The kiss was long and deep, like an intimate invasion of her very soul. When he drew back to meet her gaze, she saw no condemnation in his eyes.

"You're a smart woman, Katie. You're independent and strong and very passionate about what you believe in. That's what I admire most about you. So, no. You haven't ruined the mood. I wouldn't expect anything less."

Seconds later, after easing the condom down his length, she lowered herself onto him. The sensation was so intense her head dropped back as she gasped out his name. She felt so completely filled by him.

When he brought his mouth to her breast, all thought fled her mind, including her plan to drive *him* wild. Instead she met him thrust for thrust, each one driving home what he'd said: that he admired her strength. Her passion. Her.

Then every molecule of her body tightened, only to expand a moment later in wave upon wave of pleasure. And in that moment, she'd known only the intense release of her orgasm. And that he'd been right there with her.

Eleven

"You don't think I look too pregnant?"

As Jake pulled up to the stoplight on the way to the barbecue, he slanted a glance in Kate's direction. She was dressed in denim Capri pants—which he could only assume she'd bought as a concession to their discussion about jeans. Her pregnancy was hidden beneath an oversize white linen shirt, which she wore open over a bright red T-shirt, the sleeves rolled up to her elbows. Her hair fell in loose waves about her shoulders. Other than her pinched, nervous expression, she looked gorgeous.

It was all he could do not to turn the car around, take her home and spend all day making love to her. Man, oh, man, how he wanted to do that.

How could he want her again so soon? How could he want her at all, when she was so much the opposite of everything he normally wanted in a woman?

But he did want her. Desperately. This wasn't mere

sexual desire. This was something more. Something he'd never felt before.

He'd known it the instant he stared into her eyes and promised her he hadn't been with anyone else. In that moment he'd wanted her to believe him. To trust him.

And though he didn't blame her for not doing so, something inside him had broken when she'd reached for the condom.

The light changed and he accelerated again. "You look fine. You have nothing to be nervous about."

"Right," she muttered, her hands clenched around the bowl of salad she held in her lap. "Big work-related picnic. All your friends will be there. Nothing to worry about."

Well, he kept wishing she'd show more vulnerability. He just never would have imagined it'd be over this. "Everyone's going to love you."

She let loose a very un-Kate-like snort of disbelief. "I doubt that."

"You met a couple of these people at the wedding and a lot of the guys when they came to help me move. They liked you fine then."

"It's just that I—" she exhaled a puff of nervous breath "—I don't always make a good first impression."

When he glanced in her direction, she was looking at him with a sort of desperate need for affirmation. He tried to inject his voice with the right amount of disbelief. "Really?"

She rushed on nervously, "Beth says she thinks I come off as cold and unemotional. She thinks it makes people nervous and that—" Her expression turned suspicious. "Were you being sarcastic?"

"No."

Damn, he hoped she believed him. He hadn't meant

to sound sarcastic, but he remembered the first time they'd met, at Beth's and Stew's rehearsal dinner. She'd looked beautiful, but at the same time so coolly professional, so completely unemotional, he'd faked shivering for comic effect after they were introduced.

He never would have dreamed that beneath that icy competence lay such a sweet and endearing woman. Or such a passionate one.

"Don't worry. I'll be right there with you. You'll do fine. Just relax, be yourself, and have fun."

Her frown eased slightly. "Are you sure we have to go?"

He couldn't help chuckling at the gleam of hope in her eyes. "It's just a barbecue. Nothing to be afraid of. The Andersons host this every year and I haven't missed one yet."

"But you could go by yourself," she suggested for about the hundredth time.

"Sure, I could," he admitted, trying not to sound irked that she wasn't jazzed about spending the day with him. "But we agreed that would look strange, remember?"

"And I don't look too pregnant?" She waved aside his laughter with an impatient fluttering of her hands. "I know we have to start telling people soon. But I figure the fewer people who know I'm pregnant, the less confusing it'll be when we get divorced and Beth and Stew take the baby." A pained expression crossed her face. "I guess this is going to be confusing no matter how I look. For now, I just don't want your friends to think I trapped you into marrying me by getting pregnant."

"Well, I'm sure they won't. Mostly because it's not 1952. But also because you're gorgeous, smart and successful. If anything, they'll be wondering how I got *you* to marry *me*."

She dismissed his flattery with a roll of her eyes. "Why is it people are always telling pregnant women how beautiful they are? It's as if everyone's afraid our egos are so frail they might shatter under the weight of the pregnancy."

He looked at her as he turned onto the Andersons' street.

He had no idea why other people thought pregnant women looked beautiful. For that matter, he had no idea if other pregnant women were beautiful. All he knew was that Kate seemed to be positively glowing.

Maybe it was that she'd finally caught up on her sleep. Or maybe it was that she was carrying *his* baby.

But he suspected it had everything to do with the mind-blowing release he'd found in her arms last night. And waking up this morning to find her warm and aroused, ready to make love again.

Whatever the reason, she looked more beautiful to him today than any woman ever had.

She might be worried about impressing his friends. But the only thing worrying him was impressing her.

Just relax? Yeah, that was working.

Kate clenched a soda can in her hand and smiled past gritted teeth at the circle of women surrounding her. At least a dozen women—all wives of the men Jake worked with—had cornered her on the back deck. They'd gotten the expected barrage of questions about her and Jake out of the way early, and she only hoped she'd fielded the interrogation sufficiently. Now they were chatting about everyday things—their kids, school taxes, favorite TV shows.

She wasn't quite sure what to make of these women. They all seemed so…happy. Which, frankly, was outside her normal realm of experience. She kept looking for signs of buried resentments and repressed anger but saw none. These women seemed to love their husbands, adore their children and generally be content with their lives.

Kate was a good enough judge of character to know they weren't faking it. Which left her wondering how her view of the world had gotten so skewed. Had her years in the justice system made her so cynical about relationships? Goodness knows her childhood certainly hadn't helped matters, but surely she'd gotten over that by now. Hadn't she?

Her gaze automatically sought out Jake where he stood by the barbecue pit, drinking a beer and manning the hot dog rotation. She couldn't help remembering his words from the previous night. That he admired her strength and independence. Was it really possible that for the first time in her life, she found someone who didn't resent all the qualities she worked so hard to maintain?

Part of her wished he was here with her now, but maybe it was best he wasn't. The only thing worse than having him leave her at the mercies of all these women would be having him standing beside her, always touching her, distracting her to the point she hardly remembered her name, let alone all the details of their fake marriage.

What really drove her batty was not knowing if he kept touching her because he couldn't keep his hands off her or because he was just making sure all of his buddies bought into their marriage. Was his affectionate behavior today just another ruse to make the lie more convincing?

But every time he touched her, she practically trembled, remembering that morning and how wonderful it had felt to wake up in his arms.

Just when she thought she'd crunch her soda can in frustration, one of the women steered her away from the group, saying loudly, "You look like you could use another hot dog."

As they walked down the steps into the backyard, the woman leaned in closer and added, "Actually, you just looked like you could use a break."

Not sure how to respond, Kate mumbled an "I don't know what you mean" and hoped that would suffice.

"Oh, come on. The girls can be great, but this has got to be a little overwhelming for you," she babbled on good-naturedly without waiting for a response. "You've met probably fifty people or so. And everyone's so curious about you...Well, frankly, I'm surprised you haven't flipped out from the pressure. Just remembering the names alone would make me crazy. I bet you don't even remember my name."

"Ah...I..." But what could Kate say? She didn't remember the other woman's name.

"Lisa. Lisa Anderson."

"Ouch." Kate winced. "Forgetting the name of the hostess? That is bad, isn't it?"

Lisa laughed as they reached the buffet table set up under the sprawling live oak. "Don't worry about it. Easy mistake to make when you're trying to remember dozens of names. I only had to remember one name. Which was simple enough to do, since you're the guest of honor."

Kate stopped where she stood, but Lisa didn't notice and rambled on. "Let's see...there are plenty of hot dogs left. But if you want something else, I'd recommend the potato salad. Steer clear of that thing with noodles. I tried it earlier and it was nasty. Don't know who brought—" Just then Lisa turned and must have read Kate's alarm in her expression. "Oh dear, I've put my foot in it, haven't I? That's your dish with the noodles, isn't it?"

"No. I brought the salad." Though, in retrospect,

opening the bag of mixed greens seemed a meager contribution in light of the myriad of homemade goodies on the table. But that was the least of her worries. "I just…I didn't realize I was the guest of honor." To cover her discomfort, Kate grabbed a plate and spooned onto it a dollop of potato salad.

"Of course you are. We do this every time someone at the station gets married."

"Oh." No wonder Jake had been so insistent she come. "He said you did this barbecue thing every year."

"He probably just didn't want you to be nervous. Come to think of it, though, with all the guys that have gotten married, I guess it does average out to be about once a year. You know, it's kind of funny that Jake still comes to these at all."

"Why?"

Lisa forked some broccoli onto her own paper plate. "Well, he moved up to arson…what was that, two years ago now?" She didn't wait for Kate to answer, which was just as well, since Kate had no idea when Jake started working arson. "At the time, I told Bill he'd drift away from the station. New job, new friends. I figured he'd hang out with them on weekends."

Kate could only murmur noncommittally. It hadn't occurred to her that "the guys" Jake was always referring to weren't the guys he worked with anymore.

"Now that you mention it—" she squirted a line of mustard onto the hot dog Lisa had handed her "—I think I've only met one of the guys from the arson department. Someone named Todd who came to the wedding."

"And Todd—" Lisa held up a finger to emphasize her point "—used to work in the station. In fact, he's the one who recommended Jake move into arson once he'd made lieutenant. But that's Jake for you. He has tons of ambition—look at how quickly he moved up through the ranks—but he'd never let that get in the way of his friendships."

Kate could only nod in agreement. It had never occurred to her that Jake was relatively young for his position. Or that he'd made it to lieutenant before moving on to arson.

But she knew better than anyone how loyal and dependable he was. He'd do anything for a friend. Look what he'd done for her.

"Jake really is a good guy," Lisa was saying. "Which is why Bill and I are glad Jake *finally* found someone."

Boy, how could she respond to that without feeling like a fraud? Of course she'd felt like nothing but a fraud since she walked in the door. There was nothing she could say that would alleviate that.

"I…"

"Oh, I've embarrassed you," Lisa said, placing a concerned hand on Kate's arm. "I hope I didn't offend you. I told you I can really put my foot in it."

"No. Not at all," Kate hastened to reassure her. "It's understandable since Jake's not exactly the marrying kind." As soon as the words left her mouth, she realized her blunder and quickly added, "Before he met me, I mean."

Lisa laughed. "Is that what he told you? Boy, men have selective memories, don't they? He was always talking about how he wanted to get married."

Kate stilled, her hand poised over a tray of raw vegetables. "He was?"

"Well, sure. You know what Jake is like."

Kate forced a bright smile and nodded. If she wasn't more careful, Lisa would realize that in fact she did not know what Jake was like. And wouldn't that make for interesting station house gossip.

"Before you, he's always been drawn to women who were…" Lisa paused, obviously searching for a tactful end to her sentence.

Kate just held her breath, waiting. What kind of woman was Jake drawn to? "Women who are…" she prodded.

"Well—" Lisa made a funny face "—weak, I guess."

"Weak?"

"Women who dated him just because he was a firefighter. There are women like that out there, ya know?"

Kate still wasn't sure she did. "You mean groupies?"

Lisa shrugged. "Sure, there are women like that. But worse than that are the ones who date firefighters because they feel like they need to be rescued."

"Oh."

"Jake's such a good guy, he's always been vulnerable to that kind of woman. I guess maybe all firefighters are to some extent. They love being heroes. Thankfully most of them grow out of it pretty quickly."

"But not Jake?" Kate couldn't help asking, even though she was afraid she wouldn't like the answer.

Lisa smiled broadly. "Not until you." She continued to ramble while she filled her plate with foods, blissfully unaware of the chaos her words had caused inside of Kate.

Not until you.

By marrying her, Jake was rescuing her. As surely as if he'd rescued her from a burning building.

In his eyes she needed saving. Just like all the other women he was attracted to. Once this was all over with and her job was secure, he'd realize she didn't need to be rescued. And then where would their relationship be?

Kate tried to keep up her end of the conversation, but

inside, her heart was…well, not breaking—nothing that dramatic—but her heart was definitely crimping. And she couldn't figure out why.

Their marriage was a business arrangement. Nothing more.

That was the rule *she'd* set out.

She certainly didn't harbor any secret hope about this marriage lasting beyond the six months they'd initially agreed on.

Did she?

Did it matter that Jake's ideal woman just happened to be the opposite of her?

No. Absolutely not.

Not one tiny little bit.

But he darn well could have mentioned it before now.

Twelve

"So, you had a good time?" Jake prodded gently.

"Absolutely."

He and Kate had left the party over an hour ago, and Kate had yet to give more than a one-word response to any of his questions. In the car he'd assumed she was just tired. But now that they were home, he realized something more than that was going on.

She was in full, closemouthed lockdown. And for the life of him, he couldn't figure out why.

"You seemed to get along fine with the other women."

"Hmm," she murmured in response.

Even when he hadn't been by her side, he'd kept a careful eye on her, watching for signs she was flailing about in the water, about to go under. He'd seen none.

In fact, the whole afternoon she'd seemed open and friendly, if nervous. The antithesis of how she seemed now as she stirred the milk she was heating on the stove.

"Lisa seemed to like you," he pointed out.

This time she didn't answer, but for an instant she stilled and her hand clenched the wooden spoon she held. Then she began to stir the milk at a more furious pace. When he tried to run his hand down her arm, she deftly stepped out of his way.

Exhaling loudly in frustration, he propped his hip against the countertop beside the stove and crossed his arms over his chest. Ducking his head slightly to study her expression, he said, "Do you want to talk about—"

"No."

Damn, she was not budging an inch. She wouldn't talk to him. She wouldn't let him touch her. Apparently, as far as she was concerned, he couldn't do anything right. And he didn't even know what he'd done wrong.

He pushed himself away from the counter and stalked over to the fridge for a Shiner Bock. He twisted off the top and shot it across the kitchen into the trash can.

Well, he'd tried. No one could say he hadn't.

Logic told him to take his beer to the living room, turn on the TV and veg out until she was over with whatever snit she'd worked herself into. Every scrap of common sense he had told him to just let it go.

But he couldn't do that.

He took a long draught of beer, then said, "You might as well come right out and tell me whatever's got you so pissed off, 'cause right now you're acting like a real pain in the—"

She spun around to face him, a flash of anger in her eyes. "You want to know why I'm angry?"

"Isn't that what I just said?"

"Fine. I'm angry because you should have told me you wanted to get married."

He paused, beer half lifted to his mouth, able only to stare at her in confusion. "Huh?"

Her voice was curt with barely suppressed emotion. "If you wanted to get married, you should have told me. I shouldn't have had to hear it from Lisa today at the party."

He studied her through narrowed eyes. "We are married."

"Ugh!" She turned back around, gave her milk one last stir and then poured it into a waiting mug. "That's not what I meant. Before you and I got married… She said you'd always wanted to get married."

"So?" He had no idea where this was going, but at least she was talking to him now.

She stalked toward the table and yanked out a chair. "I had always just assumed you weren't interested in marriage, that's all."

"I don't see that it makes any difference whether or not I planned on getting married someday."

"Well, it does. If I'd known that, I never would have asked you to marry me."

"Why not?" Jake asked. "It's not like I had a fiancée waiting in the wings who got bumped aside to make way for you."

Kate sighed, wishing she could explain. Or that she could rewind this whole conversation and start over again. This time trying just a little bit harder to sound like a rational human being.

The truth was, it hardly mattered whether or not he wanted to get married. His lie of omission wasn't what had upset her. That was just an excuse. No, her anger was based on something much more complicated than that. Mostly she just felt betrayed. She'd believed him when he said he admired her strength and independence. But what good was his *admiration* if those weren't the qualities he found attractive? And why, for, goodness' sake, had she let herself care what Jake thought about her?

Finding out she wasn't Jake's type fueled all her insecurities. It was like walking into a new foster home for the first time all over again. Once again having her hope and anticipation—emotions she'd fought so hard against—crushed. No way was she about to tell Jake all of that. "Well, you should have mentioned it, anyway," she said huffily.

"It didn't come up. This whole thing happened pretty quickly, if I remember right. And I still don't see why this matters."

She drew in a fortifying breath, flattened her palms on the table and forced herself to meet his gaze. "It matters because it makes our marriage even more of an inconvenience."

"An inconvenience? Is that how you see this marriage?"

"Yes. For you, it has been." She held up a hand to ward off his protests. "Don't bother trying to deny it. You've turned your whole life upside down for me. And now this."

He pulled back the chair opposite hers and sank into it. "And that's why you were so angry? Because you think you've inconvenienced me?"

"Yes. I…I don't know. I suppose," she said, lowering her gaze.

"Kate, I haven't done anything I wasn't willing to do. You didn't force me into anything."

Exactly. He'd stepped in to rescue her. To be a hero. And he didn't have the faintest idea why that bothered her.

He reached across the table and nudged her chin up with his knuckle, forcing her to meet his gaze again. "I could have said no."

"No, you couldn't have." Her disappointment welled up inside of her and came out as a sigh. "It's not in your nature."

"What about you? It's not like this whole thing has been convenient for you. You're the one actually carrying the baby. And it's your job that was at risk."

At the mention of the baby, something inside her chest tightened. She didn't like to think of the baby as an inconvenience any more than she liked to think of their marriage that way. It cheapened both.

Gazing into his eyes, she saw a flicker of confusion cross his face as he dropped his hand and added, "Let's face it, neither of us got what we bargained for when we agreed to help Stew and Beth."

She couldn't help but chuckle. "That's sure the truth." His expression intensified and suddenly laughing was the last thing she felt like doing. "Don't you worry at all about…"

"About what?"

She hardly knew how to finish her thought. Worrying had become nearly a full-time profession for her. Was she sleeping right? Eating right? Getting enough exercise? Too much exercise? And then there was the granddaddy of all worries. Once she had the baby and didn't need Jake to be her hero anymore, how was she ever going to get used to living without him?

For that matter, how was she going to find the strength to give the baby to Beth and Stew when the time came?

She'd tried so desperately to keep her heart compartmentalized, Thinking of the baby, if she allowed herself to think of the baby at all, as Beth's and Stew's.

But the baby was greedy. She kept stealing pieces of Kate's heart for herself. And Jake seemed to be the baby's willing accomplice. And Kate had no idea how to stop the two of them from absconding with her whole heart.

She looked up to realize Jake was studying her, waiting for her to finish her thought.

She opened her mouth, ready to share her fears, but then snapped it closed again. What would be the point? If she told him what she was feeling, he'd only want to help. To try to make things better. To rescue her, dang it.

She stood. "Never mind. I'm just tired. I think I'll go to bed."

She waited to see if he'd respond. When he didn't, she turned and headed for her bedroom. She'd made it halfway down the hall when he spoke.

"You should sleep in my bed. You'll be more comfortable."

His words clutched at her heart. He was just thinking of her comfort. Not her desirability.

Well, she didn't need or want someone to take care of her. She'd been self-reliant for far too long for that. If she needed anything it was for someone to want her…just as she was. But Jake wasn't that person.

No, he wanted her for who she wasn't—someone vulnerable and in need of protection.

"No, thanks, I'll be fine in my own room."

She looked over her shoulder to see him propped against the kitchen doorway, his arm raised over his head, his face lowered, as if he didn't want to look at her. The stance stretched his T-shirt taut across his chest, emphasizing his sheer strength.

And yet, somehow she was left with the impression that her words had hurt him. Made *him* vulnerable.

"No, thanks," she said again, then turned on her heel and escaped into her room.

Thirteen

On Monday morning Kate awakened to find a note from Jake propped on the kitchen table explaining that he'd been called into work during the night and hadn't wanted to wake her. In some ways the news was a relief. After their discussion the previous night, she was no longer sure where she stood with him or how to face him.

Something she never had to do since he didn't arrive home before midnight.

The following day was a repeat. Except he didn't leave a note.

By the third day of the same behavior, the fears and insecurities she'd been holding at bay flooded the common sense that told her he was just doing his job.

Even as doubts about their relationship raced through her head, she was annoyed with herself for giving them credence. This was exactly the kind of weak behavior she despised. She was smarter than this. At least, she'd always thought she was.

How very disappointing to find out after all this time that she wasn't.

If Jake had been avoiding her, it was equally true that she'd been avoiding her sister. But she couldn't any longer.

Kate needed to talk to Beth.

So after work on Thursday, instead of driving to her own little bungalow near downtown, Kate headed out on Williams Drive to the community of multiacre lots and ranch-style houses where Beth and Stewart lived.

She let herself in the side door and found Beth in the kitchen, chopping vegetables to stir-fry. Something inside of her tightened at the familiar scene. Back in the days before the insemination, she'd been a frequent dinner guest at Beth's and Stew's.

When she heard Kate enter, Beth looked up from her task. Almost instantly, her face bloomed into a smile and she practically flew across the room to give Kate a hug. But all too soon, she pulled back from the hug to scowl. "You've been avoiding me."

"I've been bus—"

"You're always busy." Beth clucked disapprovingly. "But you've never gone this long without at least calling. If Stew hadn't been getting regular updates from Jake, I would have been frantic."

"I've been—" She started to voice another defense, but then Beth's words sank in. "Regular updates from Jake? He's been...what? Telling on me?"

Beth chuckled. "He's been keeping us informed. A couple of weeks after the wedding, when I realized you were avoiding me, I had to resort to checking up on you through Stew and Jake."

There wasn't even a hint of accusation in Beth's

voice. Nevertheless, guilt twinged in Kate's belly. "I'm sorry. Things have just been…"

"Complicated?" Beth wiped her hands on a dish-towel before returning to her chopping.

"Yeah, I guess."

For a moment Kate studied her sister. As always Beth had a peaceful aura about her that was only magnified by her pregnancy. She wore a simple, high-waisted dress that emphasized her growing belly. The brown curls framing her face had been clipped back with a barrette, revealing her naturally rosy complexion. No doubt about it. Pregnancy agreed with Beth. Just as mother-hood would.

By comparison, Kate felt bloated, blotchy and gen-erally incompetent. She hated the stab of jealousy she felt. Just as she always did.

With a sigh, she slipped her arms from her suit jacket and draped it over the back of a kitchen chair. Shoving aside the negative emotions, she started to explain, "It's just—"

"You don't have to explain." Beth rinsed a red pep-per in the sink and handed it and a knife to Kate. "It's only natural you haven't wanted to see me. I certainly can't blame you for feeling resentful."

"I don't feel resentful." But she found herself focus-ing on mutilating the innocent red pepper rather than meeting her sister's gaze.

"Of course you do." Beth stopped chopping long enough to rest her hand on Kate's. "After all you've gone through for me and Stew, you'd have to be a saint not to feel at least a little resentful."

Kate looked up at Beth. She toyed with the aban-doned stem of the pepper while studying Beth's expres-sion. There was no judgment there. No annoyance or frustration. Only acceptance. Which somehow only made Kate feel worse.

She shrugged. "I suppose on some level, I have been feeling a little resentful."

To her chagrin, Beth chuckled. "Well, that's a step in the right direction."

Since she'd been feeling so proud of her admission, Kate arched an eyebrow and asked, "Just a step?"

"Oh, come on, Kate. You've given up close to a year of your life for Stew and me. You're having a baby for us. Married a man who was a virtual stranger. And it turns out it was all unnecessary. Of course you're resentful. Maybe even downright angry."

Beth set down her knife and sighed. "And to make matters worse, I handled things very badly." Her voice held an unusual note of self-censure. "When we first found out we were pregnant, I was so happy for us, I let myself ignore what an awkward position I'd put you into." Her hand drifted down to her belly. "I'd forgotten that our dream come true would pretty much be a nightmare for you."

"Well, I don't know that I'd use the term nightmare," Kate said wryly. "It certainly hasn't been all negative."

She'd certainly had her share of positive experiences these past several months. The amazing feeling of having the baby move inside her. The excitement of the baby's sonogram. Living with Jake. Getting to know him and realizing he was so much more complex than she'd thought. Sleeping curled up next to him in bed. Feeling his hands and mouth bring her unthinkable pleasure. All things she never would have experienced if she hadn't become the surrogate mother for Beth and Stew.

In that light, how could she possibly resent Beth for

putting her in this position? And how could she think of her baby as unnecessary?

She loved this baby. She could never regret all she'd been going through to bring this baby into the world.

"There's been a lot of upheaval in my life," she admitted. "But it hasn't all been bad. Not by far."

"I'm glad." Beth smiled. Not her normal, peaceful smile, but one filled with joy. "And what about work? Things haven't been too rough for you there?"

Kate's hand drifted to her own belly. The silk shell she wore untucked over her black maternity pants certainly didn't hide her bulging belly. With the jacket, things were a little more inconspicuous but not much. "A couple of people have noticed, but I haven't made an official announcement or anything."

"And how have people taken it?"

"So far, everyone's been excited and supportive."

"Even Judge Hatcher?"

"Hatcher's been so busy with his campaign he's barely noticed me at all. He's still circling the McCain case like a vulture. The case won't start for another week, so we'll see if he continues to behave."

The funny thing was how unconcerned she was about the case. About work in general. Mere months ago, all of that seemed so important. So completely vital to her life. Now, work was…just work.

She took it seriously. Still did her job to the utmost of her ability. But it was no longer the focus of her life. Other things had taken its place. Her baby. And Jake.

Which brought her to the purpose of her visit. As quickly as she could, she explained to Beth what had happened between them. Beth listened in near silence.

When Kate was finally done, Beth summarized, "And now you think he's avoiding you."

"I don't just think so. He's been working eighteen-hour days. Who does that?"

Beth shot her a wry look. "You, on occasion. I can think of several times you've worked days that long. And he did warn you."

"I know. It's just…" Kate wiped her hands on a dish-towel and propped her hip against the counter. "I just can't help thinking I did something wrong. That I've messed up this entire situation and now he doesn't know how to get out of it."

"I'm sure you have nothing to worry about," Beth said. "Jake is a really—"

"I know. He's a really good guy." Kate sighed. "You're right. He is. That's the problem. That means he's not going to want to do anything to hurt me. That's only going to make him feel more—" The word caught in her throat. "—obligated to stick around."

She didn't want him to feel obligated to her. She wanted him to want her.

Just once in her life, she wanted someone to want her for her.

With a groan she propped her elbows on the counter and sank her head into her hands. "I just hate feeling so damn needy."

Beth had the gall to chuckle.

Kate curled in her fingers to glare at Beth over her knuckles. "This is funny to you?"

Beth shrugged, then nodded. "Maybe just a little." As if she sensed Kate's rising annoyance, she held out her hands in an "I'm innocent" gesture. "Not that I want you to be miserable and needy, it's just—" Beth paused, searching for a word "—reassuring to know you're not always as confident and together as you seem."

"What's that supposed to mean?"

"Kate, you're my sister. I couldn't love you more, so don't take this the wrong way. It's just that you've always seemed so very self-sufficient. Even as a kid, you never needed anyone."

"That's not true."

"Yes, it is. It's one of the things I've always admired about you, but…"

"But what?" she couldn't help asking.

"But it's a little intimidating, too. It's always made me feel a little… I don't know…" Beth gave a self-conscious laugh. "Weak, I guess. By comparison."

Kate felt her heart tighten just a little bit. This time she was the one who reached out and put her hand on Beth's. "You're not weak. You're one of the most loving, generous people I know."

Beth looked up. Her smile held just a hint of self-deprecation. "Thank you. But it's kind of nice having you here asking for advice. I've been waiting all my life to get to be your helpful big sister."

Kate raised an eyebrow. "My helpful big sister?"

"Well, sure. You've always been so independent, I've never had the chance before. I get to take care of everyone else I care about but you. I've missed that."

"I…I don't know what to say. I'm sorry, I guess."

Beth chuckled. "You don't have to *say* anything. Just keep it in mind for the future. Sometimes letting other people take care of you isn't a bad thing. It's not a sign of weakness. It's just a way of keeping the relationship balanced."

By the time she left Beth's and Stew's she felt no better about the situation with Jake. But she felt as if her relationship with her sister had changed forever.

It had never occurred to her that her sister wanted to

take care of her. That her independence deprived people of anything.

She'd certainly never set out to be aloof. It was just sort of a natural defense. At the first couple of foster homes, she'd yearned for love and attention. It hadn't taken her long to realize she wasn't going to get it. Hugs, cuddles and special treats all went to the kids like Beth. The cute little moppets with big eyes and curly hair.

In fact, there had been several foster homes that wouldn't have taken her if the courts hadn't insisted she and Beth stay together.

She'd learned early on that the only person she could rely on was herself. That was what she'd been doing ever since. Her independence—her steadfast refusal to trust anyone else—had protected her, yes. But now she wondered what it had cost her.

Fourteen

Jake didn't like to think of himself as a weak person. Hell, he supposed no one did. But Kate… Kate was his weakness.

She made him question decisions he'd made with confidence. Made him want things he couldn't have. Like her. And their baby.

For the first time in his life, he didn't just want a woman sexually. He wanted her love. Her trust.

Kate didn't trust him.

That much had been obvious the night she reached for a condom even though he promised he hadn't been with anyone else.

And she didn't trust him enough to open up to him.

Jeez, to hear her talk the other night, you'd think the divorce papers were all ready to go, just waiting to be signed. For all he knew, she still planned on filing for divorce the second Hatcher was elected and her career was safe. Hell, it was possible their time together meant nothing to her.

Yeah, it had always been in the back of his mind that this was a temporary situation, but things were different now.

Making love to Kate had changed everything.

But Kate needed some convincing. He needed to prove to her she could trust him. And, damn it, he had every intention of doing just that before making love with her again.

At least, that had been his plan Monday morning when he left the house early and stopped by the doctor's on the way into work. But getting the test results had taken longer than expected. Three days to be exact.

By Thursday afternoon, he had the clean bill of health from his doctor in hand. Just what he needed to prove to Kate that he was trustworthy.

At five-thirty, when she still wasn't home, he wasn't worried. After all, she probably hadn't left work right at five, and she might be stuck in traffic. By seven-thirty he was wearing a path in the rug from the front door to the back. Sure, she'd worked late before, but this was ridiculous. He'd tried her cell several times but either she wasn't answering or she was out of range.

By nine-thirty, he'd planted himself on a kitchen chair, midway between the two doors, and sat with his elbows propped on his knees.

When the front door finally opened at ten to ten, he no longer knew what he felt: fear, anxiety or outright anger.

When she entered the bungalow, her gaze went immediately to his. "You're home," she said, sounding a little surprised.

"You're late," was all he managed to grind out.

She frowned. If he hadn't been so annoyed, he might have found her expression of confusion amusing.

"I had dinner with Beth and Stew."

"You should have called." He didn't bother trying to keep the exasperation from his voice.

But as soon as he said the words, he knew they were a mistake. Her eyebrows snapped together and her shoulders stiffened.

"I didn't call, because I didn't know you'd be here."

Her response set the warning bells in his head ringing, but the surge of emotions roiling within him was too strong to tap down. He just couldn't keep his mouth shut.

"You still should have called."

"*You* didn't call." She crossed her arms over her chest, her gaze narrowing.

"I was at work," he defended. "You knew I'd be late."

Why were they even talking about this when all he wanted to do was pull her into his arms and kiss her? Peel off a couple of layers of clothes and spend the rest of the night exploring her body. Finding all the hidden sensitive hollows.

"Oh, right." Her voice practically dripped with sarcasm. "I was supposed to know you wouldn't be home until after midnight *three* nights in a row because on Monday you left me a note saying you'd be late."

He shoved his hand through his hair. "This isn't what I wanted to talk to you about tonight."

"Then what *did* you want to talk about? I'm sure you can come up with something else to criticize me about. But if you don't mind, I'd rather skip it tonight."

With that, she spun on her heel and headed for her bedroom.

Guilt stabbed through him. How had this gone so badly? Gotten so out of hand?

Hell, he didn't know. All he knew was he couldn't let her storm off to her room again.

He caught up with her in the hallway. "Wait."

Maybe she heard the desperation in his voice or maybe she was just as tired of fighting as he was. Or maybe he was just lucky. Whatever the reason, she stopped.

She didn't turn to face him, but merely cocked her head to the side. Under the circumstances, he was happy to get at least that from her.

"I didn't mean to…"

What? He asked himself. Act like a total ass? Antagonize you? Alienate you?

Finally, in lieu of a babbling admission of guilt, he settled for, "I was just worried."

This time, she did turn to face him. Her expression softened—just a little—but most of the anger had left her voice. "I don't need you to worry about me. I can take care of myself."

"I know." But knowing that didn't ease the powerful urge within him to protect her, to make her his.

He kept that to himself. She was so strong. So independent. She'd never approve of his cavemanlike urges. For that matter, he wasn't sure *he* approved of them. He certainly never would have pegged himself as that kind of guy.

Not wanting to reveal any of that to her, he changed the subject. "I saw my doctor on Monday."

"Your doctor?" Her forehead furrowed in concern. "Why? Is something wrong?"

He pulled the printout of his test results from his back pocket. "I had myself tested again."

He held out the folded paper, but she didn't take it from him. "I don't understand."

"Everything checks out. Got the all clear, so to speak."

Finally, she took the paper from him, but she didn't unfold it or even look at it. "You did this for me?"

"I wanted you to trust me. I wanted you to know I hadn't lied to you."

"Why?"

"Because I want you to know you can trust me. I want—"

"No." She shook her head. "Why does it matter to you?"

It took a second for her question to sink in. "Because I care about you." Since she still hadn't read the test results, he gestured to the paper she clutched in her hand. "Aren't you going to look at them?"

Kate forced herself to unfold the paper and stare at the results. Part of her brain registered the words typed on the page. The all clear, to use his term.

But most of her mind was still focused on his words. He cared about her. He wanted her to trust him.

She thought of what Beth had said just that evening. About how she was too independent.

After so many years of trusting only herself, could she trust anyone else? Could she forgive herself if she didn't at least try?

Carefully she folded the paper and handed it back to him. "Okay."

He narrowed his gaze as if he wasn't quite sure he'd heard her correctly. "Okay?"

She nodded. "Okay. I'll give it a try."

Part of her wished she could give him something more solid than, "I'll try." But he seemed to accept it for the major step it was. The hopeful smile that crept across his face was all the proof she needed that she'd made the right decision.

When he pulled her into his arms, she felt not only the familiar stirrings of desire, but also a tiniest thread of fear. This was all so new. So fraught with emotional sand traps. But she shoved her fear away, burying it deep within.

She'd only said she'd try to trust him. Surely she could do that without getting hurt.

Jake woke to the smell of Kate lingering on his pillow and the sound of her showering in the bathroom.

For a few minutes he lay in bed, just listening and remembering. His erection hardened beneath his cotton boxer briefs as he thought of how responsive she'd been last night. How she'd groaned, deep in her throat, every time he sucked her nipples into his mouth. How her skin had somehow tasted both sweet and spicy. How she'd moaned his name again and again as she rode him to ecstasy.

He'd never forget what it was like making love to Kate. But there was one memory that he'd cherish even more. The tentative smile on her face as she told him she'd trust him.

For the life of him, he couldn't figure out why she got to him in a way no other woman ever had. Maybe it was because she was the mother of his child. But he didn't think that was it. That alone, he could have understood.

But this crazy compulsion he felt not just to make love to her but to protect her and be with her, to dig through the layers of her personality until he really knew her, that was what he couldn't understand.

Until he did, he was more than willing to sublimate all the other stuff for the one urge he *did* understand. The urge to make love to her. To imprint himself on her, body and soul.

He rose from the bed and made his way to the bathroom. Once inside, he realized she was humming so softly, it could barely be heard over the water. The room was thick with steam and the scent of her lavender shower gel.

For a moment he closed his eyes, remembering how he'd once pictured her in a bubble bath, her skin moist and warm from the water, the crests of her breasts just visible above the bubbles.

Someday, once the baby was born, he'd make love to her in the tub, but for now Kate naked in the steamy shower would do.

He stepped out of his boxers. Her eyes popped open at the rattle of the shower curtain against the rod. A faint smile curled her lips as she watched him step into the shower.

Shampoo bubbles mounded on her head. Beads of water clung to her eyelashes and skin, converging into rivulets that sluiced down her chest. Her nipples were hardened, dusky pink against her creamy skin. Her hips swelled gently out from her waist, which still appeared surprisingly narrow given her growing belly.

He wouldn't have thought it possible, but he felt his erection swell even more. Only then did he realize he'd never seen her naked before. Not in the daylight. Not when he could really look at her.

He felt a ridiculous surge of pride as he stared at her ripe body. After a minute, he sensed her stiffening. His gaze returned to her face to find her smile had faded.

"Believe it or not I used to be quite fit."

Part of him wanted to laugh at her obvious insecurity over something he considered so beautiful. But he knew better. *That* would get his butt kicked out of this shower faster than anything.

Instead he closed the distance between them and

cupped her jaw in his hand, urging her to look in his eyes, to see the truth of his words.

"No woman has looked more beautiful to me than you do right now."

"Yeah, right. I'm a real pinup girl. Big hips, bulging belly—"

He pressed his lips to hers to stop her babbling. Despite whatever fears she might be harboring, he felt her mouth melt under his, her body sway against him. The swell of her belly brushed against his erection, sending pleasure arching through his body.

He had to force himself to pull away from her embrace. He did so only because he desperately wanted her to believe him.

"You said you'd trusted me."

A flicker of hesitation flashed through her eyes. Then she nodded. "Yes."

"Then trust that I won't lie to you. Ever."

She seemed to be searching his gaze, looking for insincerity that he knew she wouldn't find.

His hand slipped down to caress her belly. "You can't imagine how the sight of you turns me on. Seeing you like this, knowing that I did this to you, that this is our baby…it's the most erotic thing I've ever seen."

Her mouth once again curved into a smile. A little hesitant. A little bashful. But still so achingly sexy he could hardly stand it.

Once again he pulled her to him, to make her trust his words with his touch. He poured all of his pent-up emotion into his kiss, to let her feel the power she held over him.

With gentle and loving hands he tipped her head back, rinsing the shampoo from her hair. His fingertips followed the trail the bubbles left across her shoulders, down the arch of her back and over the swell of her buttocks.

Her head tipped back exposing the length of her neck to his mouth. Her skin was warm and moist and tasted sweet, like fresh rainwater. He could spend a lifetime kissing this neck. Feeling her pulse leap beneath his lips. Hearing her moan his name. Running his hands across her silky smooth skin and cupping the weight of her breasts in his palms.

He wanted this moment to last forever. He wanted to imprint it on his memory. But an even stronger force drove him on—the urge to make her his, to push himself into the moist folds of her flesh and to bury himself deep inside her.

His hand slipped farther down her body. His fingers burrowed through her curls to the sensitive skin that lay sheltered between her legs.

Her legs parted, granting him access, and he quickly found the hardened nub. Massaging her with his thumb, he sank his finger deep inside her. A low moan tore through her, and he felt her orgasm building with every stroke of his thumb.

He held her in his arms as she trembled with her release, watching every flicker of ecstasy that crossed her face. Knowing he'd brought her to that state gave him a surge of pleasure, as well.

As the last shudders of her orgasm pulsed through her body, he murmured, "I want to be inside you."

"Yes," she gasped. "Now."

He started to reach behind her to turn off the water— they could be in his bed in mere minutes. But before he could, she turned around. Bending over, she planted her hands firmly on the shower wall.

He didn't need more encouragement than that. Nudging her knees slightly apart, he sought and found her entrance. He plunged into her with a single thrust. They both moaned aloud.

The pleasure was so intense, at first he could hardly move. She arched her back, urging him deeper. He slipped his hand around her to once again find her nub before thrusting into her again and again. Her moist folds seemed to cling to him, massaging his shaft, bringing him pleasure unlike anything he'd ever experienced with another woman.

Not that he even remembered another woman. Not when he had Kate. It was only her. Only the water pounding on her back to the rhythm of their movements. Only the thrusting of her hips bringing him closer to ecstasy. Only the feel of her clenching around him. Driving him over the edge.

The intensity of their joining left him shaking. And shaken.

Because with her, it wasn't enough.

It would never be enough.

Fifteen

They'd been sleeping together every night for almost a week now. Ever since he brought home those test results.

He wanted her to trust him, he'd said. And part of her did. She trusted that he would never hurt the baby. She trusted that he wouldn't intend to hurt her. And she trusted that he wanted to be with her.

But she knew better than anyone how temporary desire could be. It was as transient as love or affection. In less than four months, she'd give birth, Beth and Stew would take custody of the baby, and this would all be over.

What would her life be like then?

Probably she'd go back to the way things had always been. Her, all on her own. Completely independent. Protected from life's disappointments and pains because she never let anyone close enough to hurt her. Once she would have sworn that was exactly the way she wanted things. Now it just seemed terribly lonely.

How could she go back to that life now that she'd experienced a baby growing inside of her? Now that she knew what it was like to sleep with Jake curled against her back?

She thought briefly of the McCain divorce that was on her docket for Monday. For years, everyone in Georgetown had seen them as the perfect couple. Well matched in every way. They certainly hadn't started out their relationship intending it to end in a messy divorce. No one ever did.

The thought disconcerted her so much, the comfort of Jake's sleeping embrace started to feel smothering.

As gently as she could, she slipped out from under his arm, but the extra weight of the baby made her clumsy. Before she could exit the bed, Jake was awake.

"What do you need?" He raised up on his elbow, his gaze clear and alert in the darkness.

"I was just going to…" What? Escape to the other room to brood in peace? Fret endlessly over their future? She fumbled for an explanation and finally finished lamely, "…get a glass of milk."

"You're thirsty?"

Thirsty? Panic-stricken? Sure, those were about the same. "Yes."

He rolled off his side of the bed. "I'll get it for you."

She started to follow him, but he stopped her. "No, stay here. I'll bring it back for you."

Before she could protest he started propping pillows behind her and helping her to sit up in bed. "You want milk or something else?"

How about your love?

Oh, crap. Where had that thought come from?

"Milk will do."

She watched him leave the room with a sinking feeling in her gut. Then she flopped back against the pillows and pressed her hands to her face.

"How about your love?" she muttered to herself.

God, she was a mess.

She didn't really want him to love her, did she?

And it certainly wasn't as if she loved him.

Did she?

She didn't give herself time to search her heart. No. She didn't. She wouldn't be that stupid. Not when she'd spent her whole life being so smart when it came to her emotions.

"Here you go."

She pulled her hands from her face and opened her eyes to find him standing over her, a tall glass of milk in hand. "Thanks."

He handed her the glass, then sat beside her on the bed. "Hey, what's wrong?" he said, running a hand up her arm.

A shiver of awareness followed in the wake of his caress. She wanted nothing more than to set the glass of milk aside and lose herself in his touch. To let him banish the worries that kept her up. To make love with him until she was too exhausted to remember all the reasons she was on a collision course with emotional heartache. She didn't let herself do any of those things.

She did, however, avert her gaze. "If it wasn't for me, your life would be a lot easier."

After being in the kitchen, Jake's eyes hadn't fully adjusted to the dark of the bedroom, making it impossible for him to read her expression. But he could hear in her voice that something just wasn't right.

Once again, he marveled at her complexity.

So tough one moment, so vulnerable the next.

There were a hundred things he wanted to say to her. None of them she was ready to hear.

So he settled for, "If it wasn't for you, I wouldn't be about to become a father."

"You're thinking about keeping the baby?"

"Even if I agree to let Beth and Stew raise her, I'll still be a father. After this, I can't imagine not being a part of her life. Can you?"

Instead of answering his question she said, "If you agree? So you are thinking about keeping the baby?"

"You can't tell me you haven't thought about it."

"I…" She frowned, pulling away from his touch. "What do you want me to say? That I'm tempted? Of course, I am. But I know Beth and Stew will be better parents for this baby than I could ever be alone. For that matter, either one of them would be better than I would."

"I disagree."

Obviously frustrated, she swung her legs over the other side of the bed and stood. "It's a moot point. There are two of them and only one of me."

He stood, as well, and caught her in his arms as she rounded the bed. "But there are two of us."

Even in the dark, he saw her gaze widen. "What are you saying?"

What *was* he saying? That he wanted them to be together?

Yes, it was what he wanted, but did *she* want it?

Come on, Morgan, you want to be in the game, it's time to ante up.

"Let's stay married. Let's raise this baby on our own."

He heard her sharp intake of breath. For a second she seemed to be actually considering it. Then she shook her head and pulled away from him. "Oh, Jake, I don't know."

He felt a sharp stab of disappointment. He'd wanted… What? Surely not a declaration of love from her. A little enthusiasm maybe.

But she hadn't said no. Which meant he still had a chance of convincing her.

"What's not to know?" He cradled her face in his hands. "We're good together."

"Sure, in—"

"Not just in bed. In life. I love you. I love the baby."

She pulled away from him, turning her back on his arguments, but just before she did, something in her gaze wavered. Instantly he knew how to win her over.

"Come on, Katie. You care about the baby, too. You can't deny it. She's *our* baby. We can be a family together."

He ran his hands across her shoulders, down her arms, praying his touch would be more convincing than his words.

She stiffened at first, as if to reinforce her defenses against him. Then slowly she relaxed, leaning her back lightly against his chest.

"Okay," she finally whispered. "Let's do it."

He pulled her fully against him, wrapping his arms around her chest. Beneath one palm, he felt the pounding of her heart. Beneath his other lay the baby that had brought them together...and convinced her to marry him.

He'd hated playing that card. Hated manipulating her like this. But not as much as he hated the thought of losing her.

It was day one in the divorce proceedings of the most important case of her career. And all she could think about was Jake.

He didn't really love her. He'd just said that.

How could a man like him—someone who loved being a hero and rescuing people—really love a woman like her? She was the last person in the world who needed saving.

Agreeing to stay married to him had been an extremely stupid thing to do. But how could she resist when he painted such a compelling picture of their future together?

She could see it so clearly in her mind. Lazy Saturday mornings making love with Jake. Lazy Sunday mornings around the kitchen table, she and Jake sipping coffee, a towheaded toddler sitting on his lap, gumming a waffle.

She was on the way from her chambers to the court, smiling at the images in her mind, when the first wave of pain washed over her.

Immediately she put a hand to the wall to brace herself and grasped her belly with her other hand. Her stomach felt unnaturally hard beneath her palm. The muscles taut and cramped.

The pain seemed to last forever before slowly easing. The whole time, she'd breathed out sharply through her mouth. Praying the sensation would pass. Praying this wasn't a sign something was terribly wrong.

As the last of the pain dissipated, she pressed her back against the wall, needing its support to catch her breath. Even after she was breathing normally, she found she couldn't move.

Her heart began pounding, her fear threatening to overwhelm her. Something was wrong. Something was *very* wrong.

She glanced down the hallway toward her chambers. There was a sofa. She could lie down. Drink some water. All of her pregnancy books seemed to recommend drinking water when things were wrong. And call Jake. He would know what to do.

But then her logical mind scoffed.

Yes, he would rush to her side. Be there in an instant

if she needed him, but would having him there really be any more helpful than drinking a glass of water?

She looked to the other end of the hallway. Just beyond a pair of double doors was her courtroom, where the McCains, their lawyers, and a myriad of reporters and sundry people were waiting for her.

All she had to do was walk the twenty meters her courtroom. Then she could spend the next four hours sitting comfortably in her chair. She could drink all the water she wanted.

She'd almost convinced herself it was the right thing to do when Kevin rounded the corner and spotted her leaning against the wall. He practically ran to her side. "What's wrong?"

She forced herself to straighten away from the wall, moving cautiously, terrified the pain would return.

"Nothing," she said, but her voice sounded strained, and Kevin didn't look like he bought it.

"I find you leaning against the wall, gasping for breath, and you say nothing's wrong? Talk to me, Kate. Something's not right."

The concern in his voice tore at something deep inside of her and she felt her fear give way to tears. Furiously she blinked them away. She would not cry. She was not that weak.

"I felt a…" She struggled for the right word. Not wanting to admit, even to herself, how badly she'd felt. Or how badly she wanted Jake there with her. "Tightening. In my belly. I just had to catch my breath."

Kevin's eyes never left her face, but a deep furrow formed between his eyebrows. "A tightening? Isn't that the word women use to describe labor pains?"

Oh, God. Was it?

"I don't know. How do you know?"

"Two sisters. Five nieces and nephews." He placed a hand at her back. "Come on, let's get you back to your chambers. You can lie down on the sofa while I call the doctor."

The thought that something might really be wrong terrified her, so, she automatically protested. "No, it's nothing. It's passed now." She stood up straighter, to prove to herself and him that nothing was wrong. "Besides, it's probably just those fake contractions, right? What are those called? Hicks something."

"Braxton Hicks? Yes, you may be right. But your doctor will know for sure."

"But the trial—"

"Kate, no," Kevin chided, steering her toward her chambers when she would have headed toward the double doors. "The trial will wait."

"But—"

"Stop being so freakin' stubborn. Nothing is more important than this."

He was right, of course. Yet somehow, giving in to him meant admitting something might really be wrong. Despite that, she allowed him to lead her down the hall and into her chambers.

"What's your doctor's number?" he asked, flipping open his cell phone.

She stopped herself just short of giving him Jake's number first. Yes, Jake would rush to her side, but what if this really was just Braxton Hicks contractions? Wouldn't it be better to wait until she knew if she needed him?

As she rattled off the doctor's number, she lowered herself to the worn leather sofa. The moment she sat down a second wave of pain coursed over her stomach. Automatically she curled onto her side, cupping her belly in her hands.

Kevin crouched beside her. "When was the first one?"

At first she couldn't answer. She was panting for breath as fear and pain overwhelmed her. Finally the pain subsided. "I don't know." It seemed as if time was stretching endlessly. As if a lifetime had passed since she left her office. But logic told her it had been mere minutes. "What time is it now?"

He glanced at his watch. "Nine-o-eight."

She'd left for court with a few minutes to spare. "Maybe ten minutes. Maybe a little longer."

Kevin's frown deepened and he snapped the phone shut. When he spoke, his voice was so deliberately calm, she knew how worried he was. "It's still probably nothing, but I'm taking you straight to the hospital."

She wanted to protest but then thought of what Beth had said about letting people take care of her.

But Kevin was right. Nothing was more important than the baby. Certainly not her stubborn pride.

So she let him help her up from the sofa. "My purse and briefcase are in the bottom desk drawer. Can you get them for me? And you'll need to find my bailiff, Celia, and let her know what's happening."

"I'm on it." He dashed behind the desk to grab her bags and met her by the door. "What else can I do?"

"You can call Jake and have him meet us at the hospital."

and crossed to his side. Nodding toward the bathroom door, he whispered, "Taking a shower. The doctor gave her permission after dinner. She was having trouble relaxing."

"Is she—" The words caught in his throat. Nearly an hour had passed since he got her voice-mail message, his fear multiplying with every passing minute. He cleared his throat and started again. "She's okay?"

Stew nodded. In his eyes was a mixture of sympathy and censure. "The on-call doctor says she'll be fine. The baby, too." The censure seemed to win out, and he asked, "Man, where were you?"

All the disapproval in the world couldn't make him feel any worse than he already did. "I came as soon as I got the message. But I was out of cell phone range all day. I tried calling Kate's cell as soon as I got the message, but—"

"The nurse made her turn it off," Stew finished for him. "Something about the equipment." He nodded his understanding but didn't really look any more convinced of Jake's innocence than Jake felt. "Anyway, now that you're here, I'm going to take Beth home. It's been a long day."

A few minutes later Stew led a sleepy Beth from the room. Her expression was even less forgiving than Stew's had been. Jake could only imagine how Kate would react to him finally getting here.

But it didn't matter. She was safe. The baby was safe. She could be furious enough to throw things at him. As long as she was safe, he'd happily take it.

After only a few minutes of pacing, he heard the click of the bathroom door opening behind him.

He spun around to see Kate framed in the doorway. She was wrapped in her bathrobe, her hair clipped high on her head a few damp tendrils trailing her neck.

Something inside of him seemed to break at the sight of her. He didn't even try to restrain his urge to hold her, but rushed across the room and pulled her into his arms.

"Oh, God, I was so worried." He pressed a quick kiss to her lips before pressing his cheek to hers. "I've never been so worried in my whole life. But Stew said the doctor said you and the baby would be okay."

Only then did he realize how stiff she felt in his arms. It was like holding a stranger, rather than holding his wife. He pulled back to search her face.

"You *are* going to be okay, aren't you? The doctor—"

"We're fine." She pulled away from him and walked around him. "The doctor wants to keep me here overnight. Just to keep an eye on me. But the baby should be just fine." Clutching the robe tightly across her chest like a shield of armor, she sat on the edge of the bed.

Seeing her, alive and apparently healthy, did little to ease his anxiety. He needed to keep touching her. He crossed to the chair Beth had vacated and laid his hand on Kate's knee. "Oh, Katie, I'm so sorry I wasn't here. I just got your first message—" he glanced at his watch "—about an hour ago."

"It's fine." She moved her knee from under his hand and swung her legs onto the bed.

"There was a fire outside of Jarrell. It looks like someone started it to cover up a homicide. We were up there all day. Out of cell phone range."

"It's fine," she repeated.

But when he reached for her hand, she slid it under the blanket. Further proof that it was, in fact, not at all fine.

"Katie, if I'd known, I would have been here hours ago. I just didn't get the message."

Finally she looked at him. The sparkle that normally lit her eyes had faded. "Don't worry about it. Kevin was with me."

Now that he thought about it, the first of the phone calls had been from Kevin. He didn't know if he should be thankful that Kevin had been there for Kate, or jealous as hell.

Next time, Jake vowed, she wouldn't have to depend on anyone else but him.

"From now on, I want you to carry the dispatch number with you at all times. They can reach me when my phone is out of range."

"That's not necessary. You don't have to be at my beck and call."

The chilly tone in her voice made him almost as nervous as all the don't-touch-me signals. "Yes, I do. That was the point of us getting married. So I could be here if you needed me."

"No, the point of us getting married was to protect my job."

Maybe he had that coming. After all, he didn't mention that mere days ago he'd asked her to stay married to him for the baby, and for love.

"I thought we agreed things are different now."

She continued as if he'd said nothing, "While we're on the subject of my career, we don't really need to worry about me losing my job anymore."

Unsure where she was going with this, he said, "That's good. But why?"

"The McCain case will have to be reassigned to someone else. And even Judge Hatcher wouldn't fire someone on medical leave. He wouldn't get much political mileage out of that. And by the time I'm back at work—"

"Whoa. What do you mean medical leave?"

"The doctor wants me on bed rest. Probably only for a few weeks, but possibly for the rest of the pregnancy.

He's got me on terbutaline, too, to stop the contractions but wants me to stay off my feet."

He sank back against the chair. "You said you and the baby were okay."

"We are okay. And between the bed rest and the terbutaline there's no reason why I can't carry to term."

"But there's a possibility you'll require bed remainder for the rest of the pregnancy?"

"Worst case scenario, yes."

"But that's like four months."

"Which is exactly why I asked to be taken off the McCain case. It wouldn't be fair to have them wait."

"I'm not worried about the case. I'm worried about you." Again he tried to take her hand. Again she pulled away from him. "Your work is important to you. Are you going to be okay with this?"

She gave a faint little laugh, with just a hint of sorrow in it. When she met his gaze, her expression seemed resigned rather than sad.

"Funny, work just doesn't seem as important as it used to."

Even though she obviously didn't want to be touched just now, he couldn't resist brushing her hair from her forehead and pressing a kiss to the spot of skin he'd bared.

"We'll get through this, Katie. I can take time off, if I need to. Or we can hire someone to stay with you during the day. Or—"

"No, Jake. That's what I've been trying to tell you. We don't need to get through anything."

His gut seemed to drop about a foot. "What are you saying?"

This time, her expression was emotionless. "There's no reason for us to be together anymore, Jake."

"Katie—"

"We got married to save my job. But my job isn't an issue anymore."

"What about us?"

"There never really was an 'us.'"

"No. I don't believe that." Unable to just sit there listening to this, he stood and paced to the windows that lined the far wall of the room. "We were going to try to make this work." He turned around, searching her face for any sign that this was tearing her apart as much as it was him. "We were going to be a family."

"I know. I'm sorry," she said, looking away. The breaking of her voice over the word *sorry* was the only sign she felt anything at all.

"No." He paced back to her. Gripping her chin between his thumb and forefinger, he forced her to meet his gaze again. "Sorry isn't good enough. Talk to me. Why are you doing this?"

"I just think that—"

She yanked her chin from his grasp and twisted to stare blankly at the closed door. She seemed to be struggling, either for words or for the strength to say them. Without meeting his gaze, she continued, "I'm not the woman you want."

"That's ridiculous. I—"

"No, it's not." Her eyes slowly filled with tears. "You only married me because you thought it was the right thing to do. You said so yourself. You want some woman you can take care of and protect. Who you can be a hero to. But I'm not that woman."

He couldn't stand to watch her cry. To watch strong, brave, independent Katie cry. "You're wrong, Katie. I don't want some woman I can protect."

"Lisa said—"

"Damn it, forget what Lisa said. Lisa doesn't know what I want in a wife."

"Are you sure *you* know?"

"Look, maybe I did used to date women who are different from you. But what does that have to do with anything? I don't want to be married to some woman who expects me to save her. Why would I want that? That's the kind of relationship my parents had and it didn't work out for them. The only woman I want is you."

Somehow, he thought if he just kept talking, he'd find the right words. He'd say whatever it was she needed to hear to convince her. But she was slowly shaking her head.

"No, you don't. You want someone who will be a good mother. Someone who—"

"Katie, you'll be a great mother." She shook her head, but he didn't give her a chance to protest. "Is that what this is about? That somehow you're afraid you won't be a good mother?"

"I just don't have the instincts to be a good mother. I certainly don't have the genetics for it."

"Being a good mother is more than—"

"Today, when I felt the first labor pains, I almost didn't come to the hospital. I wouldn't have on my own. I was going to try to go to court, but Kevin found me in the hall and made me come in. The doctor said—" Her voice broke and she had to struggle to regain control. "The doctor said I got here just in time. If I'd waited much longer, it might have been too late."

The anguish in her voice tore at his heart. Damn it, he didn't care if she didn't want to be held. He sat on the edge of her bed and pulled her into his arms, cradling her head against his shoulder. To his surprise, she let him. "But you didn't wait. You came at the right time."

"Only because Kevin was there." She sucked in a

deep breath and all but sobbed against his shoulder. "I was just so afraid. I didn't want anything to be wrong. I never want to be that afraid again."

He pulled back to search her face. "So this is about you not wanting to be afraid?"

"Before all of this, I was so in control. I knew exactly what I wanted out of life. I had it all planned and everything was working out just the way I wanted it to, and now…"

"And now what?"

"And now, I just don't know anymore. But I do know I never want to go through anything like that again."

He had no idea what might calm her fears. Or even if there was anything he could say. "All I know is that I love you. I can't promise you'll never be that afraid again. I can't promise that things even worse than this won't happen further down the road. But I believe we can get through anything together. If you really trusted me, Kate, you'd believe me."

couldn't blame him for it. He had no control over cell phone towers or spotty service areas.

Still, she never wanted to feel that way again. So desperate to be with someone she loved. So afraid he wouldn't be there someday.

No, it was better—much better—to end things now.

Shoving aside her grim thoughts, she searched for something to occupy her mind. She didn't want to wake Jake, so TV was out of the question. She flicked on the small reading light beside her bed. Jake didn't stir. As quietly as she could, she crawled from the bed to retrieve her briefcase from the corner of the room. Surely there was something inside she could read.

The only folder inside contained her notes from the McCain case. She'd read them before. There was really no reason to reread them. Certainly not now that she'd be removed from the case.

And yet, when she returned to bed, she flipped through the pages with a sort of morbid curiosity. Now that she wasn't presiding over the case, she allowed herself to become emotionally involved in the unfolding story in a way she hadn't the previous time she read it.

The McCain divorce wasn't that different from any other she'd presided over in her years on the bench. The couple had married young, had a few children, whom they both seemed devoted to. Success and wealth had taken their toll on their relationship, but there was tragedy, as well. No two people climbed the ladder of success at the same rate, so their competitive natures strained their relationship. The poor health of their youngest child seemed to be the straw that broke their relationship.

In the end they simply hadn't loved each other enough to weather life's disappointments.

For the first time in her career, Kate was looking at

a case not from a professional point of view, when she'd have to decide who was responsible for what and divvy up any assets or children. Instead, she found herself wondering: if the McCains could do it all over again, would they? Was whatever joy their relationship had brought them worth the heartache they were living through now?

She had no way of knowing. And yet… She knew the statistics as well as anyone. Nearly fifty percent of all marriages ended in divorce. She also knew that many of those people married a second or even a third time. Even after living through a tough divorce, most people were willing to risk getting hurt again. Apparently even those people who'd been hurt the worst by love were willing to try again.

So why couldn't she?

She looked over at the chair where Jake was sleeping.

All this time, she'd thought she was being so smart for trying to protect her heart. Now she couldn't help wondering, was she smart or merely a coward?

Hadn't she told Jake she would try to trust him? And yet, at the first opportunity, she'd doubted him and pushed him away.

She'd always thought of herself as so fair, but she hadn't been fair to him at all. She hadn't been honest, either. She'd never even told him she loved him.

Almost as if he sensed her watching him, Jake slowly opened his eyes. It seemed to take him a moment to focus on her face. She quickly looked away, hoping he hadn't seen in her gaze how disconcerted she felt.

He moved to her side. "How do you feel?"

Nervous, confused. "Fine," she said aloud. "Just fine."

"You slept okay?"

She forced a bright smile. "Great."

"Despite the fact that you were up before six doing work?"

She tried not to look too guilty as she shoved the incriminating files back into her briefcase. "Okay. Not great. But good enough."

There was no way he'd get her to admit how much she'd missed having him in the bed with her. How tempted she'd been to wake him in the night and ask him to just lie beside her. No, if she couldn't sleep without his arm draped across her stomach or nestling her breast, then that was her problem.

Since he seemed to be waiting for her to speak, she added, "It's a strange room, and…"

"And you were worried," he finished for her.

"Yes." Though *worried* barely began to describe her mess of emotions. *Worried* was just the tip of the iceberg.

Before she could say more, there was a knock on the door. Without waiting for a response, a nurse swung open the door and rolled in a sonogram machine on a squeaky cart.

"Oh, good, you're up already," chirped the nurse, as if the sound of all that equipment being wheeled in wouldn't have woken them if they hadn't been. "That makes this easier."

Kate had spent most of the previous day being poked, prodded and generally provoked. So she was already used to having no privacy.

Jake, however, crossed his arms over his chest and scowled at the woman. "Is this really necessary at this hour?"

"Absolutely." Nurse Cheerful smiled sweetly. "Just as soon as we get a good sonogram, we'll do some paperwork, and have her ready to go when the doctor stops by to do one last check."

"But—"

Kate gently grabbed Jake's arm. "It's okay. They only wanted to keep me overnight. My doctor will continue to monitor my condition."

Before he could protest more, Nurse Cheerful had whipped aside Kate's gown and was squirting cold blue gel all over her belly.

Since this was her fourth sonogram, Kate was familiar with the process. Blue gel on her belly plus the plastic wedge-shaped wand equaled cool black-and-white shots of the baby.

No matter how aloof she tried to remain, she couldn't help but feel a jolt of excitement every time she caught a glimpse of the baby's face or a delicate hand opening and closing. Today was no different. Except today, Jake was with her.

Nurse Cheerful flipped on the machine and unceremoniously began rubbing the wand over Kate's bared belly. As she worked, the nurse rattled off a series of questions: Have you felt the baby moving today? Have you felt any more contractions?

Kate answered without really paying attention. She kept glancing from the sonogram monitor to Jake. She hardly knew which brought her greater joy—the flickering images of their baby or the expression of absolute awe on Jake's face.

At first he could only stare in openmouthed wonderment. Then finally he murmured, "My God."

She couldn't help smiling a bit at his open amazement. It so completely reflected how she felt. Without even considering the consequences, she slipped her hand into his and gave it a squeeze.

He pulled his gaze away from the monitor for a second to stare at her, but a flicker of movement on the screen snagged his attention.

"Is that a hand?"

The nurse moved the wand to home in on the tiny hand. "Yup. And she's moving her fingers. That's a good sign." She moved the wand and the hand slipped out of focus. The image on the screen shifted to include a roundish black splotch, which was divided in two and twitching rapidly. "Heartbeat's nice and strong. Give me a minute and I'll have her heart rate for you."

"That's her heart," Jake mused, squeezing Kate's hand. "That's her beating heart."

Kate tore her gaze from Jake's face to watch the screen. It didn't look like much, but somehow it was one of the most beautiful things she'd ever seen. Their baby was alive and healthy despite all she'd been through.

"Her heart rate is 142. That's good. Pretty relaxed for the day she had yesterday. Looks like you've got a pretty tough little girl on your hands. She's a strong one."

Jake's gaze jerked to the nurse's face. "It's a girl?"

Instantly the nurse turned red. "You kept referring to her as 'her.' I assumed you knew."

"No." Then Jake pinned Kate with a stare. "Did you know?"

"No. But I kind of had a gut feeling, remember?"

Again, Jake squeezed her hand. "Yeah. I remember."

The nurse seemed to recover quickly from her faux pas. "Well, your baby girl certainly seems healthy. The doctor will review this when he gets in. Otherwise, I think we're about done here."

Before Nurse Cheerful could hustle off, Jake stopped her. "Can we see her face?"

The nurse shot him an odd look.

"I haven't been to any of the other sonograms," Jake explained.

Understanding dawned and the nurse went to work searching for a good view of their little girl's face.

As she watched Jake, Kate felt guilt burgeoning within her. She'd had the first sonogram at seven weeks—long before Beth and Stew dropped their bombshell—to confirm the viability of the pregnancy. At that sonogram, Beth and Stew had been with her and it had never occurred to anyone that Jake might be interested in attending. As soon as she'd arrived at the hospital yesterday, she'd had a sonogram to make sure the baby was okay, but he hadn't been there for that one, either.

At eighteen weeks, she'd had a routine anatomy sonogram. She purposely hadn't mentioned it to him. Having him come to doctor's appointments with her seemed entirely too intimate. Too much like what real married couples expecting a baby did.

Now she realized what her defensiveness had deprived him of. An irreplaceable opportunity to see the child he'd helped to create. A child who'd always been his to keep.

His hand was warm and strong around hers. Each time he tightened his grip on her hand, she felt a complementary tightening around her heart.

She looked from his face to the gray-scale face on the screen. The baby opened her mouth to yawn, then curled her tiny fist up to her mouth and popped her thumb inside.

As she sat there, watching her husband watch their daughter sucking her thumb, Kate realized the horrible answer to her question. She was a coward.

But she didn't want to be one anymore.

Eighteen

Jake watched the nurse wheel the sonogram machine from the room with a mixture of excitement and dread.

On the one hand, he wanted to be alone with Kate. To hold her in his arms and talk about the joy of seeing their baby girl's face for the first time.

On the other hand, he couldn't blame her for no longer wanting to be with him. He'd promised to protect her, sworn she could trust him. And he'd let her down. She might never be able to forgive him.

If she still wanted to get a divorce, he'd honor her wishes. After he did everything in his power to convince her she was wrong. But he knew how stubborn she could be. He'd have to act fast.

"Kate, I—"

"Jake—"

They both broke off at the same time. She laughed nervously, but laughing was the last thing he felt like doing.

"You go." She clasped her hands together on top of the blanket in a posture that was—for Kate—practically demure. But she didn't meet his gaze.

This wasn't good. Not at all.

Maybe it would have been polite to let her go first, but screw polite. He was pretty damn certain he didn't want to hear what she had to say. No way was he going to give her the chance to blow him off before he could say his piece.

"Look, Kate, I know you have this whole list of reasons why we should get a divorce, but I think you're wrong."

"Jake, I—"

"Just hear me out. It's only fair that you hear all the reasons why we should stay married."

"But—"

"Come on, Katie, you're nothing if not fair."

She opened her mouth as if to protest, then just shrugged. "Okay, but—"

He didn't give her a chance to launch any more protests. "Things are going to be tougher now than they were before. Even if you hire someone to be with you during the day, you can't hire someone to be there twenty-four hours a day. That's just not feasible. I can be there in the evenings and on weekends."

He studied her expression, looking for any sign she might be receptive. A little frown had settled onto her forehead.

Okay, so she wasn't convinced yet. He'd just have to press on.

"Plus, there's your job to think of. Hatcher could use our divorce against you. He could even use your need for medical leave against you. You don't know what he's capable of."

Kate's frown deepened. "Those are the only reasons you think we should stay married?"

Ah, crap. This wasn't working.

"Well...no, of course not." Okay, Morgan, think. What would convince her? What did she care most about? "Obviously, there's also the baby to think of."

"The baby," she said flatly.

"Sure. If we take care of you, we take care of the baby. And a healthy baby is what's most important to both of us, right?"

"Yes, of course." But he couldn't help notice her hands clenching and unclenching on the blanket over her belly. "You're absolutely right." Suddenly she flipped the covers back and swung her legs over the side of the bed. "I'll go ahead and change. That way I'll be all ready to go when the doctor comes by."

He watched in confusion as she gingerly walked toward the bathroom. She'd almost made it there when he stopped her.

"Whoa. Hold on a minute. Did I miss something?"

"No, not at all."

"So did you just agree we should stay married?"

"Your arguments were very persuasive."

"But did I persuade you?"

He held his breath waiting for her answer. So much was riding on it. So much more than she knew. This wasn't about her job. It wasn't even about the health of the baby. This was about their whole future.

How funny that mere weeks ago, she'd had to convince him to get married and now he was desperately trying to convince her to stay married. And all he could do was wait for her answer and try again if it was "no."

For a long moment she just stared at the floor and

said nothing. Finally she turned to him, her eyes brimming with tears.

"Everything you've said makes sense. But no matter how much we both love this baby, she's not enough to base a marriage on. Not a real marriage anyway. Not the kind of marriage I want."

"What kind of marriage is that?"

"A marriage based on love."

Jake felt as if his heart skipped a beat and he had to suck in a deep breath. "Are you saying that's what you want in *a* marriage or that's what you want from *our* marriage?"

He couldn't take his eyes from her face as he waited for her to answer. It was all he could do not to stride across the room, pull her into his arms and try to coax from her the answer he so desperately wanted.

But he made himself stand still. The time for persuasion was past. Now he just wanted the truth.

"I want both," she said finally, her hand drifting to her belly. "It's great that you love the baby, but that's not enough for me. I need you to love me, too. Really love me. Not just say you do. Because I love you. Goodness knows, I tried not to. But I—"

She was in his arms, his lips moving over hers, before the next words could make it out of her mouth. As they kissed he was painfully aware of the delicacy of her condition. So he poured into the kiss all of the tenderness he felt. All of the love. Because he wanted her to know—unequivocally—how much he loved her.

He brushed his lips across hers one final time, then ended the kiss. Cradling her face in his hands, he gazed down into her eyes, willing her to believe him. To trust him.

"Yes, I love our baby. But I love her even more *because* she's our baby. She's a part of us. And I love that she's a part of you, because I love you." Kate's eyes widened slightly and her lips started to curl into a smile. "If it hadn't been for our little girl, I may never have had the chance to fall in love with you. But I love you—and will always love you—because of who you are. Not because of the baby."

Whatever else he might have said, she cut off by rising onto her toes and pulling his mouth down to hers. She kissed him with none of the tenderness he'd shown, but plastered her mouth and body against his. If she felt delicate or frail, she didn't show it in her kiss.

And her love? That was definitely in her kiss. The pure emotion there left no room for doubt.

Finally, she pulled back just enough to smile and say, "I do believe you've convinced me."

"I know you might have trouble trusting me. But that will never happen again. I promise. And I—"

"Jake, it's okay. Last night, you said you couldn't protect me from everything. And you're right. No one could make that kind of promise."

"Kate, I—"

"I know you'll protect me when you can, but there will be things you can't protect me from. There will be things I can't protect you from, either. The important thing is that we don't let those things drive us apart. If we keep this baby and stay married, yes, there's potential for all kinds of things to go wrong. But there's also potential for all kinds of wonderful things, too. I think I'm finally willing to accept both."

Jake met her gaze, his eyes filled with love and hope. "So you really want to give this marriage a shot? You want to keep our baby?"

In love there was so much potential for pain, but there was potential for great joy, too. It made her so happy, knowing she could make him happy.

She nodded. "I do. We'll need to talk to Beth and Stew of course, but yes, I do." Offering up a tremulous smile, she added, "Jake, all this time I thought I couldn't be the right woman for you because you wanted someone you could rescue."

"But—"

She stopped his words with a finger to his lips. "The thing is, it turns out I do need you to rescue me. I need you to save me from myself. Without you, I might have spent my whole life hiding from life. But now I'm ready to face anything. As long as I have you."

A knock sounded. Then the doctor strolled into the room without waiting for an answer, without even looking up from the clipboard he held open in his arm. "Well, everything here looks good, Ms. Bennet."

By the time the doctor looked up, Kate had stepped out of Jake's arms, but still held his hand in hers. "Actually, it's Mrs. Morgan."

The doctor glanced down at his chart in confusion. "But it…ah, I see. Jake Morgan is listed here as the father." He looked up at Jake. "That's you?"

Kate answered before he could. "Yes. We're the parents. She's our baby girl."

Then she slanted a look in Jake's direction that said much more than that.

* * * * *

WHAT HAPPENS IN VEGAS...

Shock! Proud casino owner
Hayden MacKenzie's former fiancée,
who had left him at the altar for a cool
one million dollars, was back in Sin City.
It was time for the lovely Shelby Paxton
to pay in full—starting with the wedding
night they never had....

His Wedding-Night Wager

by **Katherine Garbera**

On sale February 2006 (SD #1708)

Also look for:

Her High-Stakes Affair, March 2006
Their Million-Dollar Night, April 2006

Silhouette® Desire®

Coming this March from

MARY LYNN BAXTER

Totally Texan

(Silhouette Desire #1713)

She's only in town for a few weeks…
certainly not enough time to start an
affair. But then she meets one totally
hot Texan male and all bets are off!

On sale March 2006!

From reader-favorite
Kathie DeNosky

THE ILLEGITIMATE HEIRS

A brand-new miniseries about three brothers denied a father's name, but granted a special inheritance.

Don't miss:

Engagement
between Enemies

(Silhouette Desire #1700,
on sale January 2006)

Reunion
of Revenge

(Silhouette Desire #1707,
on sale February 2006)

Betrothed
for the Baby

(Silhouette Desire #1712,
on sale March 2006)

COMING NEXT MONTH

#1711 CAUSE FOR SCANDAL—Anna DePalo
The Elliotts
She posed as her identical twin and bedded a rock star—now the shocking truth is about to be revealed!

#1712 BETROTHED FOR THE BABY—Kathie DeNosky
The Illegitimate Heirs
What happens when coworkers playing husband and wife begin wishing they were betrothed for real?

#1713 TOTALLY TEXAN—Mary Lynn Baxter
He's the total Texan package and she's just looking for a little rest and relaxation.… Sounds perfect—until their hearts get involved.

#1714 HER HIGH-STAKES AFFAIR—Katherine Garbera
What Happens in Vegas…
An affair between them is forbidden, but all bets are off when passion strikes under the neon lights of Vegas!

#1715 A SPLENDID OBSESSION—Cathleen Galitz
She was back in town to get her life together…not fall for a man who dared her to be his inspiration.

#1716 SECRETS IN THE MARRIAGE BED—Nalini Singh
Will an unplanned pregnancy save a severed marriage and rekindle a love that's been stifled for five years?

SDCNM0206